Life and Public Services
of an Army Straggler

Life and Public Services
of an
ARMY STRAGGLER

By Kittrell J. Warren

Edited with an Introduction by
FLOYD C. WATKINS

*UNIVERSITY OF GEORGIA LIBRARIES
MISCELLANEA PUBLICATIONS, NO. 3*

UNIVERSITY OF GEORGIA PRESS
ATHENS   1961

Paperback edition, 2010
© 1961 by the University of Georgia Press
Athens, Georgia 30602
www.ugapress.org
Printed digitally in the United States of America

The Library of Congress has cataloged the hardcover edition
of this book as follows:
Library of Congress Cataloging-in-Publication Data

Warren, Kittrell J.
   Life and public services of an army straggler.
      98 p.
      1. United States—History—Civil War, 1861-1865—Fiction. I. Title. II.
Series: University of Georgia. University of Georgia Libraries. Miscellanea
PZ3.W25317 Li
61-17536

Paperback ISBN-13: 978-0-8203-3479-0
ISBN-10: 0-8203-3479-0

Contents

Foreword

Kittrell J. Warren was a little known Georgia author whose literary output in book form is limited to three small volumes. All of them are rare, there being seven recorded copies of a *History of the Eleventh Georgia Vols.*, . . . three of the *Ups and Downs of Wife Hunting*, and only one of the *Life and Public Services of an Army Straggler*. In addition to being the rarest of his works, *An Army Straggler* issued under the pseudonym Chatham, is his most important contribution to literature. In it is combined the popular type of humor of the period with the sinister character of the deserters from the Confederate Army, one of the sorrier aspects of the Confederacy.

Although, as our able editor states in the Introduction, *An Army Straggler* is not a document of either great historical or literary value, we believe that it deserves a wider use among those interested in Southern literature than the one copy in the University of Georgia Libraries can provide. It, therefore, is being issued as the third number in the University of Georgia Libraries Miscellanea Publications.

W. P. Kellam, Director
University of Georgia Libraries

Introduction

THE heroism of the soldiers of the Civil War has been celebrated in a vast number of diaries, journals, memoirs, poems, and novels. But realistic and comic treatments of Confederate and Union soldiers are not so abundant. Stephen Crane's common soldier and raw recruit, Henry Fleming, is more human than epical, but even he overcomes his cowardice and achieves a flag-waving heroism. And the career of this deserter was created in fiction nearly thirty years after the war by an author who was born six years after the end of the conflict. Kittrell J. Warren's *Life and Public Services of an Army Straggler* is unusual because it is a fictional treatment of the exploits of an army deserter, written by a Confederate soldier and published only a few months after Appomattox. Warren was probably the first veteran of the war who wrote comic and realistic fiction about the Civil War. This book is also a rarity because there is now only one known extant copy.[1]

Warren was born in Alabama in 1829. His family moved to Houston County, Georgia, and then to Lee County in 1837 or 1838. At various times in his life Warren was a lawyer, a legislator, a county judge, a newspaper columnist and editor, a Confederate soldier, and a writer of pamphlets. On July 3, 1861, he enlisted as a private in the Confederate Army.[2] That

[1] Though Miss Ella May Thornton listed *The [sic] Army Straggler* in her *Finding-List of Books and Pamphlets Relating to Georgia and Georgians* (Atlanta, 1928), p. 119, it is now impossible to determine where or how she learned that such a book ever existed. The only copy now known to be extant is the autographed copy purchased by the University of Georgia Library from Walton Folk in 1958.

[2] An inaccurate and brief sketch of Warren's life is given in his obituary in the Atlanta *Constitution*, December 29 (Sunday), 1889, p. 17. See also Floyd C. Watkins, "Introduction" to Kittrell J. Warren, *Ups and Downs of Wife Hunting, Emory University Sources and Reprints*, Series X, No. 1. When I edited this work, the only known extant copy was a second edition in the Emory University Library. Late in 1957 James Morgan Hale, of Atlanta, Georgia, discovered and purchased a first edition, which was printed in 1861 in Atlanta by Franklin Printing House; Wood, Hanleiter, Rich & Co.

same year he published *Ups and Downs of Wife Hunting,* a
comic pamphlet on courtship, a sort of jokebook for Confederate soldiers. A result of his military service was a *History of
the Eleventh Georgia Vols., Embracing The Muster Rolls,
Together with a Special and Succinct Account of the Marches,
Engagements, Casualties, Etc.* (Richmond, 1863). His third
and last book-length work was the story of *An Army Straggler.* Thereafter Warren dabbled in his legal and journalistic
careers. He was editor of various newspapers, and he wrote
columns usually in the vein of eighteenth-century gossipy
essays or of the burlesque sketch popular among the humorists
of the Old Southwest. When he died in 1889, *An Army
Straggler* was his sole significant achievement in literature,
and it was already forgotten.

Despite Warren's grandiloquent and patriotic Preface and
some oratorical and sentimental flights within the story, *An
Army Straggler* is not a celebration of a glorious lost cause. It
is, actually, almost the opposite of that: a comic treatment of
the unsoldierly deserters and stragglers who preyed upon the
country instead of defending it on the field of battle. Though
Warren sympathetically portrays the sufferings of civilians
in Virginia, his main focus is on a Confederate rogue. Warren
assumes a realistic rather than a sentimental or patriotic view;
he is a humorist and something of a social historian rather
than an orator at a gathering of Civil War veterans. And there
is a sound historical basis for his narrative. In September,
1864, Jefferson Davis said that over one third of the army
was absent without leave.[3] Warren's hero-villain-deserter, William Fishback, is a fictional representation of no less than a
hundred thousand Confederate deserters.

Fishback has, therefore, a grounding in historical fact.
That is not to say, however, that he is an accurate portrait
of an individual or the class of deserters and stragglers. He is
a poor man's Johnny Reb, the lowest common denominator
of all the bad aspects of a deserter in a civilian and democratic
army. He is a depraved example of the unsoldierly traits of
what is now called the GI or the dogface. He is the Sad Sack
of the Civil War running amuck. But he is more than this
too. Fishback is the picaro, the rogue of the old picaresque
novel adapted to fit the American Civil War scene. And a poor

[3] Ella Lonn, *Desertion During the Civil War* (New York, 1928), p. 31.

white rogue at that. Indeed, he is the descendant of the poor whites described in William Byrd's account of Lubberland. He is a close relative of George Washington Harris's Sut Lovingood, Johnson Jones Hooper's Simon Suggs, and Augustus Baldwin Longstreet's low characters like the dirt eater Ransy Sniffle, whom Warren mentions in *An Army Straggler*.

Before the Civil War, the Southern humorists generally created vigorous and realistic red-blooded American backwoodsmen and pranksters and rogues. The local colorists who succeeded them after the war were nostalgic. They saw the world sentimentally, and their tinted spectacles caused them to see a beneficent glow in the roughest characters. The tall-tale-telling frontiersmen were replaced in the new era by Mary Noailles Murfree's rough-looking and tender-hearted mountaineers, Thomas Nelson Page's old Southern Colonel, and Joel Chandler Harris's village philosophers. *An Army Straggler* is interesting and significant because it is one of the last remnants of Old Southwest humor. It looks backward to Davy Crockett, Hooper, Harris, and Longstreet and vaguely forward to later uses of frontier humor by such diverse writers as Mark Twain, William Faulkner, and Robert Penn Warren. Fishback's shrewdness provides comedy in the same way that the ignorant Will Stockdale's horse sense does in Mac Hyman's *No Time for Sergeants*.

Most of the devices which Warren uses in telling his tales are either derived from the conventions of the Old Southwest humorists or based on characters who resemble those backwoodsmen known by the earlier Southern writers. William Fishback is the famous ugly man of the old tales. As a child, writes Warren, he enjoyed "a long and beautifying spell of the mange." He is a consummate liar, a prankster, and a practical joker in every situation. Unlike Sut Lovingood, who lies and enjoys pranks for the pure love of lying and jokes, Fishback is a utilitarian liar who tells his lies and tricks other characters strictly for his own advantage. Though he is sometimes himself the victim, he usually triumphs or gets revenge. Fishback has absolutely no conscience, not even the Robin Hood ethics usually found in the picaro. "Prove to me," Warren writes, "that the memorable Patriarchs of the antideluvian [*sic*] world dressed in the present Parisian fashions and chewed tobacco for a livelihood—establish the fact Julius Cesar [*sic*] was a woman—Cicero an idiot and Napoleon Bonaparte a chunk of fat light-wood—and then possibly, but not till then, will I be ready to admit that—far down in the hidden depths of Fishback's soul, there might still have floated some shattered fragments of a wrecked and stranded Conscience." This lack of a moral feeling, or, indeed, a moral order, is in keeping with most writings by frontier humorists. Warren does, however, make a gesture toward poetic justice by letting Fishback die of smallpox at the end of the yarn.

Warren's styles, techniques, and dialect are typical of his predecessors. Most of the humorists of the Old Southwest were gentlemen, or they posed as gentlemen and social historians, recorders of the mores and customs and speech of wild and unruly frontiersmen. Like Longstreet and Joseph Glover Baldwin, especially, Warren begins and ends the episodes of his yarn with digressions, moralizing tags, high-flown rhetoric, oratory, and glances at literature and history. Warren is a self-conscious and old-fashioned narrator; frequently he intrudes to serve as the civilized frame of an episode or a chapter. He invades his own story with pompous and comic digressions, he displays his knowledge of literature in numerous allusions and quotations, he utters disclaimers, and he uses his own personality to provide contrast and perspective. The pretentious Captain Slaughter uses polysyllabic words which counterbalance Fishback's dialect; the Captain is in some respects a forerunner of the King and the Duke of *Huckleberry Finn*.

The folkish and comic rascality of the character of William Fishback is Warren's greatest accomplishment in *An Army Straggler* and actually in his entire career. Fishback's homely and exaggerated figures of speech are worthy of the best folk humor in dialect. One horse trots hard "enough to churn the chittlins outen a feller." A muddy road is "the saftest kind of batter." To Captain Slaughter, Fishback offers "a nip at this canteen—hit's got some uv the peore tally-twisty [tail twister?]: hit'l brighten a feller's caracter jest to rub up agin it." When Fishback proposes to a girl, modestly she tells him that he's not in earnest, that he prefers a Georgia girl. And tactfully he replies to the maiden: "Drat the infernal Georgy gals, they ain't fit to tote guts to a bar!" Money, Fishback observes as he tries to steal from Slaughter, is "mighty slippery, hit's got wings bigger'n a buzzard, now a days, and flies away without flappin em, silent as a cat." When Fishback poses as a doctor, a soldier asks if he has any medicine. "None," he replies, "ondly a little ligmy cognum [laudanum], I carry along to cure the scours." Sometimes Fishback's ignorance is dumbfounding. When he hears a sorry parody of Poe's "The Raven," he calls it "a regular ripsnortin good hyme. . . . Hit's what you mout call a real buster." Warren attempts to indicate humor and comedy with absurd misspellings (such as *goze* for *goes, noin* for *knowing,* and *rale rode* for *railroad*). This device can be effective in illiterate letters written by uneducated characters, but Warren achieves more confusion than humor with his misspellings because he uses them so indiscriminately.

An Army Straggler is not a document of great value to the modern historian; nor is it a noble work of literature. But it is a remarkable achievement for Kittrell Warren. It is particularly interesting because it was written when the Civil War was immediately in the past. If the *Straggler* does not place Warren beside Longstreet, Hooper, Harris, and better-known humorists of the Old South, it does indicate that he inherited more of their talents than did other Southern authors in the years following the Civil War.

THE TEXT

Life and Public Services of an Army Straggler by Chatham was published anonymously by J. W. Burke & Co., Phoenix Printing House in Macon late in 1865. The copy in the University of Georgia Library has *129* written in red ink on the outside cover, indicating possibly that copies in the edition were numbered. This copy is 5⅜″ by 8⅝″, with 90 pages, sewn, bound in a pale pink or peachy-buff paper cover.

Warren has written an almost illegible inscription to an unknown editor on the inside of the front cover:

This work comes to you with much incorrect typography—
If you notice it [that is, review the book] please express
to me at my expense your paper doing so [that is, the issue

which carries the review] & if I can get employment with
my pen in your city write me. Also let me know what
another edition of this work per 1000 can be published for

Yrs &c

K J Warren
Starkville
Lee Co
Georgia

Apparently Warren never published a second edition. The
appendix promised in the text was not included, and probably
the "Sequel to the Straggler" mentioned in the Preface
never appeared in print.

Typographical errors, about which Warren complained
in his inscription, have been silently corrected in this edition.
Because Warren sometimes wrote extremely long paragraphs
containing speeches by different characters, I have taken
the liberty of adding new paragraph divisions in order to
make the dialogue more readable.

Floyd C. Watkins

Emory University
Atlanta, Georgia

LIFE AND PUBLIC SERVICES

OF AN

ARMY STRAGGLER,

BY

CHATHAM.

◆◆◆

"It is the course of greatness,
To be its own destruction."

NABB'S HANNIBAL AND SCIPIO.

◆◆◆

MACON, GA.:
J. W. BURKE & CO., PHŒNIX PRINTING HOUSE.
1865.

This work comes to you with much incorrect typography — If you notice it please express to me at my expense your paper drawing &0 + if I can get employment with my here in your City write me — also let you know whether another edition of the work be (soo) can be published for me &c

A J Warren
Starkville
Lee Co
Georgia

PREFACE

The armies of the late Confederacy have won for themselves a fame that will descend to the last ages of the world. Infantry, Cavalry and Artillery, together with our heroic little Navy, have *all, all* done honor to human nature, by the gallantry, fortitude and power of endurance which characterized each progressive stage of the struggle that has closed.

If the Confederacy be a prodigal who has wandered from the parental roof, it is at least a noble, an illustrious, an immortal prodigal, and one that, for the earnest sincerity with which it departed, and the generous and harmonious cordiality of its return, deserves (if not the fatted calf,) at least an honorable place in the "father's house" and heart. But while the language of praise can never over-reach the merits of our Soldiery, it will hardly be denied that in the Confederate, as in all other armies, there has flourished a class of persons like those presented in the following pages. Mankind has no synonyms, and if, therefore, the great variety of characters composing a vast army contained no such specimens, it would be a miracle earth has never seen. It is unnecessary to enlarge upon this suggestion, and indeed, it has only been made for the benefit of that class of people whose vocations have kept them uninformed about the grosser elements of human nature.

It may be thought that the pompous wordiness of the individual here called Slaughter, (a resident, by the way, of another State,) is overdrawn. Those who know the man—who know how pertinaciously he refuses to say "clouds" when he can use the word "nebulae," or "winds," when he can say "Couriers of Eolus," will, on the contrary, decide that we have been afraid to trust public credulity with the whole truth.

The statement made by FISHBACK, with reference to the "flitter's havings rags in it,"[1] is odd, but that it re-happened

---

[1] Though Warren assumes that the reader will remember a well-known story about flitters filled with rags, the source is unknown.

to him, is a verity we can establish, and which is introduced as an illustration of the truth that "history repeats itself."

The by-laws, signs, etc., of the Co. Q. Society, although promised, as an appendix to this work, are withholden for reasons we decline giving just now. Bye and bye they will be forthcoming,—probably in the "SEQUEL TO THE STRAGGLER."

In conclusion, we have no apologies to render for the demerits of this Work. We made the best use we could of our "one talent." No troubles, no engagements, no want of facilities are here pleaded in extenuation of what, in us, "seemeth weak."

On the classic banks of the Rapidan, in 1863, we patiently sketched the outlines of the STRAGGLER, part of which we have since as patiently labored to fill; the rest will be published in future, or put among the Capulets, (the latter most probably) according to the direction it may receive from circumstances.

THE AUTHOR

November, 1865.

CHAPTER I

*In which Mr. Fishback,—the Hero,—is shoved gracefully in-
to the presence of the Public, and struts forward on his
career of glory.*

I *do wish* I could introduce my hero in a fashionable
manner.—Yea, verily, I would like to present him sumptuously
appareled, reclining gracefully upon a magnificent ottoman,
—just resting from the delicious employment of reading (that
trans-anthropean specimen of splurgery) Macaria. I would
have him a grand looking character. Intellect should beam
from his lustrous eye, and nobleness peep forth from every
lineament of his features. Nature should be in a glorious
good humor, smiling graciously upon his first appearance.

Sweet breezes—excuse me,—delightful zephyrs, and pleasant aromas should woo him. I would have the sun retreating
in good order into the fortress of night, followed by a Regiment of clouds and leaving "Sentinel Stars" under command
of the Moon, as officeress of the guard to hold the position
he was evacuating.

A spring near by, should be bouncing up out of the
earth, like an infant in a baby-jumper, and canaries—yellow-
hammers, mocking birds, crows, pigeons and black-birds,
should be croaking, chirping, and chattering in concert
around him.

Near by would sit a female,—and *such* a female! Powers,
at the sight of her, would emancipate his Greek Slave, and
throw sculpture to the dogs.

The dear young creature, with her new Sunday coat on,
and her ring embedded fingers, I would have discoursing
him on the characters of Zenobia, Artimesia, Penthesila, and
Charlotte Corday, all delivered in pretty book-talk-style, while
to the foolish, useless and ridiculous affairs of practical life,
her conduct would seem to say,—"Get thee behind me,
Satan."

In a word, fair reader, my hero should come before you,

in a style calculated to produce a favorable impression at
first sight, if I could exercise my own option in the matter.
But Truth forbids the pursuance of this course. Truth, that
scrupulous and exacting tyrant, who is always passing edicts
requiring the tongue and pen to become wheelbarrows, and
roll off the burdens of the heart and mind,—Truth—to which
my conscience, (ruling me as doth a termagant wife her
hen-pecked husband) has rendered me a conquered and loyal
subject—requires that I should present him in a far more un-
presentable manner.

Then, with your permission, *we* will commence. With a
rather well favored, though remarkably black face, and a
stout, robust frame, wrapped in comfortable looking jeans
wallowed the immortal William Fishback. The muddy earth
of Manassas, was his bed, the descending mists his vapory
and gauze-like covering. It was the 9th of March, 1862.
Johnston's army had begun the retreat towards Orange.
Troops were filing by, but our hero, who was wriggling,
twisting and distorting his countenance into all possible Comic-
Almanac shapes, seemed wholly unconscious of passing events.
"Oh Cap'n," said he, speaking to Captain Smith, a kind-
hearted officer, who bent over him,—"these here rumaty panes
is a souzin into my very inards. What on yearth's a gwine
to becum o'me; oh, oh, oh, I'me a—oh—a most ded, oh,—reckin
I'de as well go and get berried, oh."

"I'm very sorry for you, Billy," said the Captain, "I tried
to get you on an Ambulance, but the doctors say they are
every one crowded full of the sick. You know it is impossible
for me to stay with you. Take these pills, they will ease you
for a while, then hobble over to that house yonder; the
family have agreed to take you in there, and I have no doubt
they'll nurse you kindly. If the Yankees follow us they won't
trouble a man in your situation."

So saying he handed Fishback twenty-five dollars and a
pass from the Surgeon to travel at will, and hurried on. Left
to himself, our hero arose to a sitting position, still wearing a
woe-begone look for the benefit of all whom it might concern,
and soliloquized after this manner: "Cuddent stand to be a
marchin along whar all them waggins is a beatin the rode into
the saftest kind of batter, stickin myself in the ground every

step like a darnd liberty pole, slippin down every time I go
to go up and down hill, which the hills is slipperier than a
ingyun with the peelin off, and havin a officer all the time
devlin me to close up. Thar ain't nothin intisin in no sich,
least ways I haint got no hankerin after it. Cuddent let me
in none o' thar ambulanches; sed they was cram'd chuck
full ov sick uns, and yonder goze one now with four strappin,
helthy lookin youngsters, a drinkin and a laffin and a talkin
like the world was thern. Wisht I had a cannon, Ide blow em
to the fur eend ov kingdum cum. Thems sich as staze round
the big offisers, a flutterin and a buzzin like candle flies round
a candle. No mistake about it, things needs right smart
o'regalatin, but I ain't got time to stop and tend to em,
I'l be long back atter a spell." The conclusion of this sentence found him on his feet.

Starting forward he soon availed himself of the first left
hand to leave the track of the army, and moved along the
road leading to Kelly's Ford. Though freighted with a heavy
knapsack, two blankets and more than the usual et ceteras of
a marching soldier, by twelve o'clock he had made the distance of eight miles from the point at which he started.
Halting near a spring by the way-side, he drew from his
haversack a third of a pound of fat boiled middling and four
biscuits all of which he proceeded unceremoniously to devour.

As he was winding up—or more properly winding down,
—the last morsel of this delicious dinner, he thus addressed
himself:—"Well, gess ef I have no bad luck, I'll be outen
ritch uv the Yanks agin nite cetches me; then I'm agwine to
try and borry some feller's horse, get sumthin fit to eat and
maby make a forty daze furlo outen this here paper uv mine.
Wonder what the Capn would say ef he could see me now,
marched furder than he has and eat mor'n any two men in
the company. He thinks I'm a angel. Bless his old sole, he's
a pittyin uv me rite now. Wooddent bee supprized ef I
did'ent make the ole feller sweat sum uv these days, fur
not havin no better sense. Reckon this trip will pay expenses,
and likely hit'll 'fetch me a profit,' as the whale sed when he
made a reckersition for Joner. Bleeve I'll be a joggin. Spect
I'll make right smart tracks twixt this and dark. *Rumatisum!*
now haint I got a tite spell uv hit, ruther calkelate hit'll keep

a gittin wuss, twell it draws my feet into sum body's saddle sterups. Forard—make tracks, march." Dusk found him in front of an elegant mansion far down in the heart of Prince William county. Passing in at an outside gate, he proceeded through a beautiful grove of Paradise-trees to the yard, where he fell in with Major Graves, the fat, chuffy, dignified proprietor of the premises. From this "fine old gentleman," he received a generous and hearty welcome, and was ushered by him into the presence of three handsome, intelligent and musical ladies, who contributed each her share in making a display of true Virginia hospitality. Our hero, in coming in, had acquainted himself with the topography and contents of the Major's well supplied horse lot, and now that he was in good quarters, flattered with a fine prospect of becoming mounted, and petted by a trio of blooming beauties, he waxed jubilant and talked as only Fishback knew how to talk. The whole burden of his courtly phrases and elegant observations was directed at "Miss Calline" (the younger of the three,) for whom he seemed to have a soft place in his heart at first sight. "Got a heap o' monstous fine things about here aint you?"

"No, indeed, Sir," said she, scarcely able to suppress a laugh. "We are plain, unpretending people."

"Why you got a pyanner and a sofy and a heap o' sich as that."—

"Wouldn't you like to hear me play a tune?"

"I wooddent be supprized ef I mout."

Whereupon she proceeded to play several very pretty airs. Indulging in the pleasures of music and conversation, the hour of supper speedily arrived. After supper a cloud began to settle on our hero's brow. Conflicting inducements were contending for dominion over him, and he grew, of necessity, moody and silent. Neither the bewitching influence of beauty nor the charms of social intercourse could draw his imprisoned thoughts from their "dread abode." His mind was perplexed with the question, whether he should tax his weary limbs with a night's ride, or trusting the chances of waking early in the morning, indulge in a comfortable sleep. He needed repose very much, but he also needed a horse—he might by sleeping get both, or he might not.

Having retired at an early hour, he lay sleeplessly ruminating these matters in his mind, the ladies, meanwhile, enjoying sundry giggles at his expense.

At length, while yet the question remained unsettled, his attention was attracted to a conversation going on in the adjoining room. The old people were lecturing one of their daughters on the impropriety of encouraging a certain poor suitor, and warmly advocating the claims of filthy lucre, which they appeared to regard as the only "one thing needful." Gradually, women, horses, suitors and money began to whirl through his mind in such a mazy and confused waltz as soon changed them from ideals in a substantive world, to substances in an ideal. Now, oh most excellent reader, I know that heroes are generally "cut down, hewed out, surveyed and manufactured" by authors, and do not, therefore, possess a cavern in their hearts that is not penetrated and explored by these Paul Pry Knights of the quill.

Mr. Fishback is not my hero. He's his own and his country's hero. Not a creature of merry-moonshine and airy nothingness, but a mortal man of meat and muscle. You must, therefore, excuse me for acknowledging that after having wasted a large amount of time, trouble and money, in trying to ascertain his motive for so materially changing the schedule next morning, I am without a ray of light on the subject.

Perhaps his future, as developed in the forthcoming pages, or revealed by the discoveries of a scrutinizing posterity—to whom this pamphlet is presented as a keepsake—may furnish some clue to the mysterious alteration. Be that as it may, he awoke before light, purposely re-snoozed, rose with the sun, and in due time made his appearance at the table. As breakfast progressed, he essayed, with remarkable propriety, to apologize for his dullness the other evening. "I calkalate you all think monstrous curus uv my bein so serus last night, but I am in a peck o' trubble. I've jest hearn my pappy's ded. I aint got no bruthers nur sisters, and thar haint nobody to look arter the black ones—which thar is nigh on to a hundred uv em—sept mammy, and the overseer, and she's got the rickets and can't stay long—though" said he, wiping the corners of his eye,—"the overseer is mity tentive, razes

whapping big craps, and don't leve nothin ondun. Shan't
pester bout nun uv these things," sighing profoundly, "ontwell
my bleedin kuntry gits lifted outen the bog; maby next fall
I'll get a furlo and go home to have a little ritnin up"—
then turning to Miss Caroline, he remarked, "mammy's
got a pyanner and a sofy too." A mouth full of coffee, to
which that lady had just helped herself, found a sudden and
spasmodic vent, discharging itself on the contiguous portions
of the table cloth and she left the table precipitately under the
influence of a fit of something that bore no resemblance to
hypochondriasis. The old people, however, who always *know
a thing or two*, had possessed the astuteness to discover strength,
solidity and merit in the young man's character. *They understood the ring* of the true metal. From them he received a
pressing invitation to stay until the weather cleared off.
"Can't do it," said he, "can't begin to do it. Duty's my pilet,
and hit tells me to jog along. Duty! hits the word, thar's whar I
bin a standin and thars whar I mean to stick, cum jee or cum
wo. Here old miss, take yore pay outen this twenty, I aint got
nuthin littler." He was politely informed that he not only owed
nothing, but that Major and Mrs. Graves would be happy to
have him stay longer on the same terms or since that was out of
the question, to call if he ever passed again. "Thanky, thanky,"
replied our ever grateful hero. "Monstrous much ableeged to
you, shan't forget you while a drap uv blud stays under my
skin." So saying he gave to each and all a friendly shake of
the hand, and left, without having been guilty of taking anything excepting the Munchausenary privileges before referred
to.

Some ham and chicken, a number of biscuits and several
sweetcakes had entered his haversack unannounced, of which,
at the appropriate time, he made a hearty meal. A horse—the
great object of his desire was no where to be obtained. Swarms
of stragglers had for several days infested the settlement along
the road, to such an extent that all property capable of
being secreted or secured by lock and key, had been disposed of. Under these circumstances the noble Fishback displayed a magnanimous resignation to hardships he possessed
not the power to avert, and walked briskly onward. About
sunset, he pulled up at a cabin by the road side. The inmates

consisted of Mrs. Lane, a woman whose husband had been shot on picket a few weeks before, and three small children.

The ruin and dilapidation every where apparent, plainly demonstrated the fact that she, a frail and delicate creature, and one whose manner indicated she had been in better circumstances, was compelled, with her own attenuated hands, to perform all the labor done on the premises. To her he applied for rest, rations and lodging for the night. This application she at first refused, by stating that she had already been taxed beyond her ability in feeding soldiers. But he appealed so piteously that her firmness yielded and her sympathies, (there's no plumb-line can fathom the depth of woman's sympathies,) raised the latch and opened the door to our weary and shelterless hero. She told him that while any part remained of the little that was left to her, she could not send away shivering and hungry, those who were engaged in the service to which her husband had sacrificed his life. Laying off his harness, Fishback rendered himself quite useful in cutting and toting wood and feeding and watering a scrub of a horse whose visible ribs showed a sympathy in the family suffering, and a tendency to the land of buzzards.

As there was but five bushels of corn in the crib, he was informed that the horse subsisted entirely on clover, of which he would find a small supply. But doubtless actuated by motives of the purest commiseration, he furnished that needy animal a large turn of corn, carefully noted the position of the bridle and saddle and returned to the house. Supper was at length announced, disposed of, the dishes washed, and our hero, Mrs. Lane and her eldest child—the others being asleep —formed a group around the fire.

A woman's sorrows and her tongue are made companions by Nature. It is true that this companionship is often interrupted by circumstances. The heart, for instance, saddens and pines under the influence of a secret and sacred love. Then, motives of pride and a sense of duty seal this natural outlet, stop the gush feeling and thereby invoke the penalty of a violated law. Her bosom is not a place in which such prisoners can be kept with safety. Nature has issued no warrant requiring their confinement there. She bids you, my fair friend, speak forth your sorrows, that others may aid you in bearing the burdens they impose, and that familiarity with them may diminish their magnitude. She is your mother and advises for your good; reject not her admonitions. Stifle the promptings of Nature and you check the breathings of the Soul. Acting in obedience to this "higher law," Mrs. Lane soon began to ventilate her troubles.

"I feel badly that I have no better accommodations for you, but it cannot be avoided," said she. "Only two years ago, I had a father, a mother, a large and affectionate circle of friends and kindred, an affluent and happy home, and the best and noblest of husbands. A great gulf now separates me from my relations, my property has been wrenched from me by a process it is not necessary to relate and my Henry,—oh! I could have been happy with only him and my children left to me, amidst the worst visitations of Fate, infinitely and eternally happy with him and them alone. But that I might drink the cup of woe to its bitter poisonous dregs, he too has been snatched away." She wept a moment and then continued. "I shall never, never forget his parting words as he went from his home for the last time. He had come to spend but three days, and left just one week before he was killed. In separating from us he said, 'Mary, you will have hardships to endure, and no friends at hand to assist and encourage you, but be cheerful, and remember that though all else should fail, God and your Henry will forever love you.' Oh! how long and tenderly he clung to the little ones, how he pressed them to his bosom and kissed them, and when the choking tears would allow him no longer to speak, what a look of tenderness he gave me as he turned away."

These remarks were accompanied by incessant sobs, and delivered with all the pathos misfortunes could wring from the heart of a wretched woman. Our hero, who had been amusing himself meanwhile with a kitten, now threw down his broom-straw and replied, "I'm mity sorry for you, widder. Gess it'l be hard work for you to git another sich a husband. Poor widders with gangs o' pesky little brats is mity slow stock in any kind o' marryin market, now a days. But I wouldn't cry about it. Maybee some nice young buck'l take you and the young ones into his mess atter the war, thar's no noin the luck uv a louzy calf. Come, don't take on so,

yore ole man's jist the same as spilt milk, that it aint no
use a cryin over. You oughtent to take no more trubble
aboard uv yore back, nur you can kick off uv yore toze or
blow outen yore noze. Come, come, widder, thar aint no
munny in cryin, so you mite as will dry up."

These sympathetic remarks were lost on Mrs. Lane. She
understood not a word of them. She longed not for comfort-
ing words from the *kind stranger*. Her tears were now her
only comforters, and with them she was communing. "In
a few more weeks," she continued, "I will be without provisions, my neighbors are not prepared to aid me, and there
is no possible source from which I can obtain another supply.
Oh, how dark! how wretchedly dark and dreary is my future.
I could endure suffering and even starvation and death myself,
but these children, cramped with hunger and crying for
bread." Her voice ceased. Emotions of which language contains no appropriate symbols, had invaded the dominion of
speech, the eyes were uttering the liquid language of the
heart, and the tongue could say no more.

After delivering a few wholesome, practical observations
upon the impropriety of "crossin the bridge afore you get
to it," Fishback expressed a wish to retire. He had begun to
feel rather provoked than otherwise. "What did she reckon
he keered ef her darnd old husband was ded."

With this sympathetic reflection passing through his mind
our hero was shown into the next room,—a kind of shanty
attached to the house, where he found a hard shuck mattress,
lying on a coarse pine bed-stead and covered by a sheet and
two blankets, one of which Mrs. Lane had taken from her
own scantily supplied bed.—Having crept beneath the blankets,
Fishback was not long in becoming a naturalized citizen of
the land of dreams.

Sometime before day he got up, put on his clothes, took
his shoes and accoutrements in hand, passed cautiously through
the family room—the only avenue of egress—and made for the
stable. After taking the bridle in his hand he paused for some
moments as if restrained by an invisible influence, an air of
seriousness overcast his features. His bosom had become the
battle-field of contending motives. The quick-witted reader
is ready to anticipate us by conjecturing that "the silent
monitor" was urging him to refrain, and that even the re-

doubtable Fishback had not yet obtained a final discharge from the service of conscience. In this my friend, you reckon without your host. Prove to me that the memorable Patriarchs of the antideluvian world dressed in the present Parisian fashions and chewed tobacco for a livelihood—establish the fact Julius Caesar was a woman—Cicero an idiot and Napoleon Bonaparte a chunk of fat light-wood—and then possibly, but not till then, will I be ready to admit that—far down in the hidden depths of Fishback's soul, there might still have floated some shattered fragments of a wrecked and stranded Conscience. Oh no, he knew not the meaning of the word. His reason for halting was this,—the night had blown off fair and cold and he was reproaching himself for having left the blankets on the mattress he had occupied and debating the expediency of returning to get them. "Thar aint no-body thar as can harness in with a feller ef he duz git cetched," thought he—"ef the umun wakes up, I'll make her think I was a studyin so much about her sitiwation and her poor ded husband, I cuddent sleep and so had to get up and walk about. I'm glad I aint her ded husband. Dont want to be no umurn's ded husband. She dont need them blankets and ef she did some uther feller'l git them and old Bones both twixt this and to-morrer nite. I'll take keer uv em fur her. Hits my solum duty." The conclusion of this sentence brought him to the steps, he entered, crept into the room, obtained the blankets, came out, bolted the door, bestrode Bones and was off without suspicion. And now that our hero is in the stirrups, we will linger for a brief period with the occupants of the cabin.

One hour after his departure, and just before the first symptoms of morning grew visible in the purpling east, Mrs. Lane lay dreaming of her husband. He was engaged in battle. At the head of his column, his plume gracefully waving and his clear calm voice rising above the din of the conflict, moved the tall and manly form of him in whom her soul was centered. Long, fierce and sanguinary was the struggle.

Line after line, like storm-driven waves broke upon his firm column and melted away. And now diminishing numbers admonished him that the fate of the conflict was trembling in the balance.—His spirit rose to the height of the emergency. Beckoning his sturdy comrades to follow, he

rushed furiously upon the opposing cohorts. A litter soon
came from the scene bearing his dying form. His languish-
ing eyes bent on her that same look of deep and tender
affection—that look! the heart could read it, but the tongue
could not. "Mary" said he, "I am dying, I wish I could
have left you and the children better provided. For you and
them I feel the tenderest and most earnest solicitude, not
for myself. My weary limbs will be at rest. I go to a land
where death comes not, and love remains unchanged forever.
The prospect invites me away, but oh I hate to leave you now."

He gasped convulsively, remained silent a few moments,
and then, with great difficulty, continued. "Teach our dear
children to love my memory, which will soon be all that's
left of me to love. Teach them to love you, to love their duty
and their God. If they but do this, our roads may separate
here but they will come together at the end. Oh, Mary, my
Mary, we will reunite where separation—" She felt the last
pressure of the hand that held her own, for now the lips were
mute and the stout brave heart of the soldier ceased to beat.

A loud rap at the door awoke her from this dreadful
dream. She did not hasten to respond to it, but sat up in bed
weeping most bitterly. At length another and more impatient
rap hurried her up and she began to dress. But her toilet
could not be completed soon enough to satisfy the impor-
tunate and untimely visitor. His raps grew louder and more
frequent. Terrors the most alarming began to gather around
a heart already crushed and bleeding to the limit of endurance.
And now he speaks. She pauses. Her heart flutters. "Is this
too a dream, to mock my sorrows and drive me to despera-
tion." Hark! he speaks again, he utters the word "Mary."
She doubts no longer. 'Tis the voice she heard in her sleep—
the door flies open as if by magic, and the happy, happy,
happy wife melts into the arms of her yet living and restored
husband.

CHAPTER II

In which Mr. Fishback joins in a grand equestrian romp,—
Forms the acquaintance of a polite and urbane gentleman
by the name of Squalls,—Enjoys a fete-champetre in a
Cavalry camp, and disappears under a fog.

The reader is aware that the retreat of General Johnston's
army on this occasion was their second forced march, and
the first that they had performed over bad roads or in disagreeable weather. The soldiers yet continued to be luxurious
amateurs in the profession of arms. With its rigid discipline,
severe restraints and intolerable hardships, they were wholly
unacquainted. For which reason (as the veterans of that
army well remember,) the number of infantry, self-mounted,
was astonishingly great. We make this observation as prefatory
of what we are about to relate. But our business is not with
the army just now. Friend Fishback has left the trail of that
ponderous and serpentine procession, and we must bear him
company.

As we have already intimated, Bones was the only loose
horse our hero had seen since he left Major Graves'. But at
the distance of a few miles from the road horses might have
been found in abundance; horses which had *refugeed*, and
horses "to the manner born." So, while the events related
in the conclusion of the last chapter were transpiring and at
no great distance from the locality of their occurrence, two
hopeful scions of the straggling stock were decoying a couple
of steeds from the lot of a citizen. To divide their pursuers
if any, (for as yet they knew not how powerless are citizens
to check or resist the depredations of soldiers,) they determined to travel different routes. One in the direction of
Fredericksburg, and the other towards Richmond. With
no unnecessary delay, the diverging roads were taken and
the riders off at good speed. As there were a number of forks
and the way was dim anyhow, the Fredericksburg man soon
lost his route, and after blundering through the country for

some time, unconciously fell into the Richmond road a few hundred yards in the rear of his former companion, who had been delayed by the breaking of his head-stall. The Richmond man regarded himself as the object of pursuit and quickened his pace to a very respectable run. Fredericksburg, thinking that *he* had fallen into the rear of some person who had been horse-stealing, and (judging from his rapid movements,) was pursued, and not wishing to consort with any such troublesome detectives no matter who they might be after, put whip freely. Thus they moved on, over hill and plain, playing to quick time a grand John Gilpin duet. Presently a brother of the equestrian order who had been indulging in the same innocent amusement, heard their rattling hoofs behind him, and driven by the cause that drove them, labored assiduously to "preserve his interval." It was thus that one and another, and another joined the great panic-driven promenade, until the number had increased to ten, when our hero, a little after day-light heard the foremost of them closing up. Now, Bones was evidently too slow to keep "open order" for ten minutes, and there was neither place nor leisure to conceal or dispose of him. But something must be done and that in a hurry. Alighting, he was about to drop his rein and hasten into the thicket, when the pursuing horseman ascending a contiguous slope came in full view and was less than fifty yards from him. It was undoubtedly too late to escape decently and in order. But the wits of our hero did not forsake him in this trying emergency. Pretending to be an honest recapturer of the stolen horse, he stood in the middle of the road and waving his hand sang out at the top of his voice, "I've kecht him." The individual addressed understanding the remark as directed to some unseen executioner of the law, and as having reference to himself, reined up so suddenly as to make a full somerset over the head of his horse, barely touching his feet to the ground before he disappeared in the thicket. The astute Fishback, though greatly surprised at this manoeuvre, understood the cause in a moment and began loudly to berate the thief and to fulminate terrible threats for the purpose of preventing the possibility of his return. While engaged in this interesting pastime he suddenly discovered Dick Squalls, of Wheat's

Battalion, the next man in the procession, now right upon him, and denoting an unmistakable determination to pass on. This circumstance filled him with the most dreadful apprehensions that an enemy less moderate than the mild administrators of the law, was close behind, and he spoke out, "is the Yankees a cummin." "Don't know nor don't care" remarked the person interrogated, at the same time reaching out a long keen switch and giving our hero as he passed him a forcible and stinging rap across the face and breast, merely to flex and exercise his arm. Fishback, smarting and writhing under this painful and mortifying insult mounted his newly acquired horse and put forward.

From a number of reasons which will suggest themselves to the mind of the shrewd reader, without being here specifically set forth, the impression soon obtained among the fugitives that Federal troops and not civil authorities were in pursuit of them, which apprehension resulted in a slackening of their speed, (as they knew the Yankees could not be close at hand) and a closing of the column, though they still swept on at no mean rate. Wherever they went, the people along the road began to pack up and prepare to move and some fled without either packing or preparation. Many of these reached Richmond and reported Stewart's whole force in full retreat before a stupendous raid. The exciting intelligence was heralded to the world by the morning papers, borne along the wires to every part of the Confederacy, and in a few days published prominently and with a flaming caption in the columns of the New York Herald. But on sped the cavalcade, little regarding the tumult and commotion their movements excited.

At length they came in view of a company of cavalry at breakfast by the road side. A council of war was immediately held,—Squalls assumed command, and it was arranged that they should halt at the cavalry camp, report the Federals close behind in over-powering force, inquire the road to Richmond and profess to be going hither under orders of the most pressing importance. Just as they were about to begin the execution of this plan, strange developments on the part of the cavalry were discovered. Seeing a number of men halt along the road and commence conferring together within three hundred yards of their quarters, they began to indulge in some misgivings; their misgivings grew into fears; and their fears were now culminating in a grand universal panic. Squalls scanning these demonstrations with the eye of an experienced General, suddenly stuck spurs to his horse and with a clarion voice ordered his men to "charge," an order which (observing as they did the "situation") was obeyed with no little alacrity. Vainly did the officers of the company endeavor to make the men of their command fall in. "Men" said a subaltern officer, while ensconcing himself, as if by accident, in rear of a huge clay-bank, "men, rally, fall in, behave yourselves like brave soldiers, don't you see there's not more than fifty of them at the outside. Rally, rally to the rescue, and die if necessary, rather than abandon your colors." But he could not infuse his own courageous spirit into the minds of his followers. Giving heed to information communicated by a certain intelligent gentleman of antiquity named Solomon, to the effect that "a wise man foreseeth the evil and hideth himself," they fled in every direction, leaving a remnant of their breakfast, their wagon equipage, and supplies, and a considerable majority of their horses. Being now in undisputed possession of the field, Squalls admonished his men that "delays were dangerous," and ordered each to fill his haversack from the deserted breakfast and select a fresh horse with all possible dispatch. In obedience to this command it was not many minutes before they had accomplished the work assigned them and were huddled together, ready to mount and resume the march. But at this stage active operations were retarded by an unforeseen occurrence. Fishback had taken the finest looking and best caparisoned horse on the ground. Squalls insisted that as the victory was attributable entirely to his skill and generalship he deserved the pick of the spoils. Our hero always revengeful, still felt the smart of the lick he had received and of course stoutly denied the justice of this claim. Squalls avowed his determination to enforce obedience with the strong arm of power, when Fishback suddenly seizing a heavy bludgeon drove him to the earth with great violence, vaulted into his saddle and loped away. Meanwhile the boldest or more probably the slowest of the cavalry, having discovered as they retreated, that only ten men, and they dressed in grey uniforms, had composed the routing party, surrounded and captured this invading rabble just at the moment our lucky hero had effected his escape.

The infuriated Squalls was trying to mount one of the cavalry horses and pursue his fugitive antagonist, unconscious of the presence of any opposing foe, for some minutes after they had taken peaceable possession. But here, even in this embarrassing predicament, we must abandon the cause of the Squalls dynasty. Its fortunes concern not our present purpose. Before passing from the subject, however, we will state that although no blow was struck, excepting that inflicted by Fishback, yet, rumors growing out of this affair, were spread upon the wings of the wind to the effect that an accidental and terrific collision had taken place between two Confederate squadrons, in which guns, swords and bludgeons were freely used, producing frightful carnage. Another report, (and which, by the way, Squalls certifies is correct,) states that the captured party were allowed to capitulate and be paroled after subscribing the following very reasonable and moderate terms of capitulation: First, They were to be allowed to march out with their horses, accoutrements and side-arms.

Second, They were never more to disturb the quietude, molest the chattels or "fright the souls" of the aforesaid company, except under circumstances of compulsion or by virtue of a previous agreement.

Third, They were to speak everywhere and on all occasions in highly flattering terms of the gallant and determined stand taken by said company against a supposed enemy. And

Fourth, They stipulated, on their arrival at Richmond, (whither they professed to be going for orders from the War Department,) to earnestly recommend that a sick furlough be forthwith granted to every member of the company aforesaid.

As we know Squalls' tongue is somewhat tricky, we distinctly disavow any intention to endorse the statement that such a protocol or indeed any paper of any sort passed between the parties. It might or it might not. Be that as it may, this veracious biography shall no where give sanction to a doubtful assertion. But our business is with Fishback, and to him let us return.

He spent that night at the house of a citizen in Albemarle county, and left next morning in the direction of Lynchburg, after managing to worry into his knapsack, surreptitiously, a suit of cloth and a pair of gold studs. He had now formed the grand design of taking a horse-back trip to Georgia, the State of his nativity and home.

Of immortal heroes, however, as well as common people, it may truthfully be said,

"The best laid schemes of mice and men,
Gang aft aglee."

But the next three months of Fishback's history must remain unwritten for the present.

Should a gracious public warrant us in issuing another edition of this work, the seal of secrecy will then be removed, provided the causes which now silence our pen shall have ceased to exist. The inference may possibly be drawn from what has been stated, that we designed to intimate our hero was disappointed in his projected excursion to Georgia. We emphatically deny that we meant to be so understood. We were merely dropping a moral observation of general, not individual application. Our object was to envelope the period of Fishback's history, not now inserted, in profound darkness. There we have left it and there it shall remain for the present. Should any untoward mischance impose upon future developements or succeeding generations the necessity of disclosing a reliable account of the circumstances here pretermitted, we tender assurances of the fact now, that *we* are thoroughly acquainted with them all. If Fishback suffered misfortunes, *we* were present with the balm of sympathy; if he reveled in a hortus deliciarum, the gates were not closed on us; if he "played fantastic tricks," *we* were his playmate; if he went home to attend his daddy's hanging, *we* bore him company. In a word, wherever he went, *we* were *thar*. Not in the flesh, but in the *sperrit*. Whatever he did we *seed it*. Not with our *nateral* eyes, but the eyes of our inner man—those eyes that don't wear spectacles, and have never been known to need them—those eyes that have alone seen castles in the air, purity among human beings, happiness on earth, or whiskey too mean to possess a single redeeming quality.

CHAPTER III

In which the Fates are found to be in rebellion against our Hero,—His early Life and Pedigree are given, and many other interesting Discoveries made.

One evening about the middle of June, as the army lay stretched around Richmond, Capt. Smith received a letter which, upon opening, he found to read as follows:

> Cassel Thunder, June 10th, 1862.
>
> My Dear Capn,
>
> Atter you Lef me i wus sente here to the hoss spittle, whar i bin mity six every sense tother day i Hobbled out to the markit house to git a little sumthin as wood lay on my stummick when a guard tuck me up and maid dout like he kecht me a steelin Capin you no i aint no steelin carrecter, i want you to cum and git me outen here ime mity bad off which This aint no plais fur a dyin man cum quick ur ill be ded ime pourful puny and a Gittin wuss, nuthin more but remanes yours true frende twel deth
>
> William Fishback

Time was when such a letter as this would have produced both indignation and sympathy in the mind of the tender-hearted Captain, and when he would have sworn (like grand jury bailiffs) to keep himself "without meat, drink or fire—candle-light and water only excepted" until he had wrenched from the unholy clutches of the law, its innocent and helpless victim, But captains, like those diffident, girl-like creatures, called politicians, sometimes change their minds, and Capt. Smith's had certainly undergone a most decided revolution, so far as the interests of Fishback were concerned. To be plain, he had come to regard that remarkable gentleman as a most notorious humbug, and therefore, merely read the letter, filed it away and paid no further attention to its contents. We do not pretend to uphold the Captain in his ungracious deportment, but it is our duty to concede to him, a privilege to which even the worst criminals are entitled before the enlightened reader is permitted to pass sentence of condemnation against him. He must "be heard in court."

Well, then, having failed for some time after the exodus of Fishback to receive any tidings of him, and feeling great anxiety on the subject, Capt. Smith had written to Mr. Bates, of Pinderton, in Worth county, Georgia, as follows:

Camps near Richmond, May 15th, 1862.

HON. JESSE BATES,

Dear Sir—On the retreat from Manassas in the early part of March last, I was compelled to leave Mr. William Fishback sick by the road-side. Since that time I have not heard a word of him. I feel very much attached to Billy, and suffer great uneasiness about him. Please give any information you can about him, whether he is at home on furlough, or has been heard from, etc. My object for writing to you is because I have heard William speak of you often as a friend. I believe your son and he were school-fellows and inseparable associates. By replying at as early a day as convenient, you will greatly oblige,

Yours truly,

JOHN SMITH

Captain Co. —, — Ga. Reg't.

To this letter he received the following answer, which contains the only reliable information now in our possession with reference to the early life of Fishback:

Warwick, May 24th, 1862.

CAPTAIN JOHN SMITH,

My Dear Sir—Your letter of the 15th found my father much too busy to reply. In fact he has scarcely leisure to wink his venerable eyes, from the time he emerges a mensa et thoro, in the morning until he flies up to roost at night. Under these circumstances he has confided to me, his hopeful and "saft-fingered" offspring, the delicate and important duty of drafting a response. A duty which, though laborious, I hope, with the aid of a little brandy and water, to accomplish to your entire satisfaction.

Well, you want "any information" I can give you about Billy Fishback. Taking you to mean literally what you say,

I will proceed to dilate your pupils and surfeit your mind with a long letter and many important facts upon the subject of enquiry.

Bill was born in Irwin county of this State, about twenty-two years ago, "more or less." His mother, at the period of this event, was a pedestrian organ grindress, and sole proprietress of a domesticated monkey. One of her petticoats, (for I positively assert upon my honor she had two,) was converted into swaddlings for the infant and a wallet to tote him in. It was her custom, in traveling, to strap this wallet across her shoulder with the bantling Fishback in one end and a rock, or probably a pumpkin in the other, to balance it. When the baby grew fretful she would put the pumpkin, or may be it was a rock, in the same end with him that he might both play with it as a toy and enjoy its society as a companion. Time sped apace, and the infant at length emerged from his wallet—as doth a chicken from the shell—and after enjoying a long and beautifying spell of the mange, grew in stature and comeliness. But, Capt., since I am about drifting into a biographical sketch of your pet, I must not neglect a reference, brief though it may be, to the genealogical tree from which sprung this prodigious sprout. Such an omission would be unpardonable in a biographer. Your Billy can point proudly to his ancestry and exclaim with a swelling soul:

> "My ancient and ignoble blood
> Has crept through scoundrels ever since the flood."

His mother, Mrs. Fishback, descended from the illustrious family of sharpers who have so long and in the face of such formidable opposition, retained great power and influence in the City of New York. Her father, Mr. Bloomfield, was many years ago expelled from what is now known as the "Five Points," on account of conduct regarded by that orderly community as disreputable and unbecoming. After this event, he held for a long time and with great credit to himself, the office of nurse in the Georgia Penitentiary. The charming Miss Hardy was confined, I mean held to labor at the same place, and an attachment sprang up between them which resulted in a subsequent marriage, the fruits whereof were Mrs. Fishback, and several other children whose names I do not know. I believe Mr. Bloomfield to have been a good man, whose life was doomed to be made up of a constant series of persecutions for opinion's sake. He was a Socialist, and seemed to regard himself specially commissioned to execute as far as need required, the doctrines of that honored creed. He took the position that "all things are" universally admitted to be "fair in war," then he would prove to a demonstration that human life is a never ceasing warfare, ergo "all things" done in human life "are fair," *i.e.*, right. But foolish laws and ignorant jurors disregarding his sense of duty and the strong argument by which it was fortified compelled him (like our people-loving, self-abhorring politicians) to "waste the bloom of his youth in the service of the State." Upon the subject of Fishback's pedigree on the father's side, I am almost without information. His father, William Fishback, Sr., was born at some unknown locality far down in the wiregrass of Georgia, and (it is said) grew to the age of twenty-one before he ever knew that human beings were accustomed to wearing shoes on their feet. In fact of the great frisky world and its whims and customs he knew as little, as doth the ebon native of interior Africa about the sun's parallaxes. Soon after reaching his majority the elder Fishback moved to Irwin and settled in the neighborhood of a crossroads grocery. I now approach an interesting period of his life, the period of his marriage. And here Captain, I will state for your information, that marriage, like many of our greatest blessings, often comes as the apparent sequence of a venial and unnoticeable accident. A man, for example, walks rapidly along the street with his head up, reflecting on the magnitude of the universe, when suddenly he stubs his toe. The toe hurts, and he grins and makes faces over it. A woman passes along at this juncture and looks piteously at him; that look reaches the heart and he falls in love, courts and marries her. Now, to sum up; but for the accident, that his meditations were too exalted for him to look where he stepped; but for the accident that an obstacle was in the way and his toe *accidentally* collided with it; but for the accident of a woman's passing just then and looking as though she pitied him, when her thoughts, were really, in all probability, on another subject; but for this whole chapter of accidents, I say, two well yoked people might have wasted life in singleness. It was thus with Mr. Fishback. He had a great fondness for shooting game—especially hogs, cows and sheep, and indeed had acquired such celebrity for appropriating to his own use other people's stock, that he was universally designated as "appropriation Bill." It happened on one occasion, as my father says, and he lived in the neighborhood at the time, that Mr. Fishback, when about to go on a hunting excursion discovered that he had only one round of ammunition. But he knew of a neighbor who had some he could afford to spare, and thither he started. His way led by the cross-roads. On arriving there he found a considerable crowd congregated. Justice's Court had just adjourned, and judges, jurors, parties, witnesses and spectators were all bending under the weight of whiskey. A woman grinding on a hand organ and a dancing monkey occupied the centre of a ring whose circumference was lined by a full muster-roll of all persons present. He felt bewildered and amazed, such sights and such sounds he had never witnessed before. A superstitious wonder got hold of him. He rubbed his eyes to see if he was really awake, and then looked down upon himself to ascertain if it were actually he. At length all hands (the organ grindress included) were invited in to "take something." Fishback, of course, imbibed; that was one of the tenets of his faith. The drinking was followed by more playing and dancing, and the playing and dancing by more drinking, until after a while Fishback was announced as the next man in order to stand treat. In vain did he plead that his money was left at home. Everybody clamored in favor of carrying out the rules. Now, the rules which had been established before his arrival and of which, to do him justice, he was entirely ignorant, required each man, as his name was called, to either treat, marry the woman or be rode on a rail two hours. After exhausting all expedients in trying to get out of the scrape, Fishback finally selected and mounted his rail. For about twenty minutes he demeaned himself in a manner as becoming and dignified as could have been expected of a gentleman in his delicate situation, but at length four fresh hands took charge of the rail, turned up the sharp side and struck a trot. This was more than mortal man could bear. A parley was called, and Fishback consented to marry. The rail was now of course thrown down, and the rail-rider borne in triumph to the grocery on the shoulders of a whooping populace and there placed under guard until the license could be sent for and procured, when the nuptial ceremony was duly performed by a drunken Magistrate upon a drunken pair and witnessed by drunken spectators. Night had, by this time, come on, and I am informed that bride, bride-groom and attendants each slept till morning wherever she or he fell, when too drunk to stand longer. Your bosom friend and my "inseparable associate" was the fruit of this suspicious union. As before stated, Mr. Fishback's marriage was the result of a great many trifling accidents. But for his fondness for hunting—but for the scarcity of ammunition—but for the needed supply being beyond the grocery—but for the wonderful properties of the organ and the remarkable feats of the monkey—but for the "rules" established, the sharpness of the rail, the roughness of the trot, &c., &c., &c., "Billy" would undoubtedly have been numbered among the non est invent-ables. Before leaving the subject of this marriage, let me observe that I have never heard of one conducted in a more practical, business-like manner. There was no display of "sickly sentimentality or finnikin susceptibility" by either party, in fact they never spoke a word to each other until after the knot was tied. Then, too, there were no invited guests, no pomp or pageantry in connection with the occasion. There is no doubt in my mind but that the style of celebrating modern marriages is a monstrous innovation upon the rite, as originally established. Marriage is nothing more and nothing less than a bargain settled between two contracting parties, and is entitled to no more attending circumstances than any other bargain. Suppose, Captain, you offer me five hundred dollars for lot of land number thirty-six in the fourteenth District of Lee county, and I agree to make the trade, but postpone signing the deed until Wednesday week, so that I may buy a new suit of clothes—propose a feast and invite a crowd to witness the act of signing. You would go off astonished, and perhaps buy some other man's land or give out making the trade before the day appointed. Now the one is as reasonable, though certainly not as fashionable as the other. The truth is, a land trade is more binding, legally, and therefore entitled to more solemnity than a marriage. Marriages, however well solemnized, are only verbal contracts and subject to be invalidated by divorce; deeds are written and sealed, attested and delivered with all the force laws can impart to them, and (if they start right) can never be divorced, divested, diverted, nor devoured. If a crowd were present at the deedsigning, their tears would shock the nerves of no shrinking, timid female, nor would their mirth and feasting give evidence that parents were delighted because a daughter was about to be sent forth from the parental roof. But I must stop this moralizing. About ten months before the birth of William Fishback, Jr., his father took a trip to lower Georgia, from which he never returned. He died suddenly near the city of Savannah, from the effects of a disease in the neck. Upon the particulars of that solemn event, I have no information except such as is contained in the following manuscript verses, handed me by the former Sheriff of Chatham county, who attended him in his last illness:

"Old Billy Fishback's left the drive,
He's just as dead as Hector,
He's quit imbibing rot-gut rum
And gone to gulping nectar."

"He was a man of stately frame,
Of comely form and feature,
A man of mark——for cows and swine,
Not mark of Art or Nature."

"A *single line* might well suffice,
To show how he departed,
When on a Georgia platform stood,
Bill Fishback, e'er he started."

"Although the Sheriff gave him rope
And let him have a showing,
Yet, strange to say, he lost his wind,
Even while the wind was blowing."

"But now he's gone—peace to his shade,
We shouldn't wish him back with us,
But on his humble head-board write
'Bill Fishback wasn't worth a cuss.'"

The sad event so plaintively related in the above verses is, I assure you, my dear Captain, a source of great pain and mortification to me. But after stating that Mrs. Fishback is still in being, I must proceed to resume the subject of this letter, to-wit: "any information" I can furnish with reference to her son. Young William had not been long out of the wallet before he began to exhibit his insteeped depravity by stealing from the monkey the best half of that animal's rations, and using all convenient occasions to inflict pain upon him merely that he might have the fun of seeing him make "monkey motions." But with all his faults I must say that as he grew up, Bill loved his mother. Human beings, Captain, never fail to possess some waif of original purity that has floated above the wreck of man's moral nature. Some heir-loom transmitted by an unfallen Adam to even the most degraded of his posterity; some faint resemblance of the Maker's blurred and ruined image. Writers of fiction ignore this truth, but experience condemns them as slanderers of their race. Heigh! I'll have to quit this brandy, it's about to make a philosopher of me. As I was saying, Bill loved his mother, served her faithfully, and was, in some respects, a dutiful and obedient child.

Mrs. Fishback having removed to Pinderton, about the age of fourteen, her boy became a pupil of Mr. Wesley Sparrow, who taught in a gin-house, which was, therefore, called "Sparrow's High School." At this time Bill and I were school-mates, but not "inseparable associates," by upwards of a good deal. The fame of his villainy had reached me before we met, and I would as soon have cultivated intimacy with a viper. In fact, the sum total of my dealings with Billy Fishback, may be easily expressed in one brief sentence: I saw him, knew him, and whipped him.

Whether he made any proficiency at Sparrow's school, I do not know. I was so tormentingly in love just then, I noticed nothing but my sweet angel, little Hebe, who has since grown to be a coarse, lubberly gawk. But I recollect distinctly, that that was the first and last of Bill's pupilage.

Mr. Sparrow had, in early life contracted white swelling, which rendered one leg much smaller than the other. Like most persons thus afflicted, he was exceedingly sensitive about it, and could not even bear the slightest reference to

the subject. One morning, on arriving at school, he found
a man painted on the door with one leg less than an inch
in length and the other just four and a half feet—for he
measured it. Fishback being the worst boy in the neighborhood, was of course immediately suspected. He had, at various
times, whipped most of the little girls in school, and several of
them saw him standing before the door making motions of a
very suspicious character late the other evening after everybody had left. Though entirely innocent the circumstances
convicted him, and he was trounced unmercifully and expelled from school. The second morning after this event, the
Seminary, alias, gin-house, was found in ashes.

At first, there was a difference of opinion as to who had
done the burning. Some believing it had been done by Sparrow
in order to effectually obliterate the odious picture. But
suspicions thickened upon the guilty Fishback, to such an
extent that he fled the country, after having stolen ninety
dollars from my father and a gold watch from the teacher.
As the Grand Jury made this distinguished behavior the
subject of special notice, in other words, as they found a bill,
Bill was not to be found in these parts again until the Spring
of last year.* About the middle of April, 1861, he came up
bringing a good horse and buggy, plenty of money, a trunk
full of fine clothes and more than all, wearing an angry-
looking cockade. I need hardly inform you that "the case
of the State" was nol pros'd. By the way Capt. when was
the cockade regiment mustered out of service, and from what
Q. M. did they draw pay? I never understood the character
of Ransy Sniffle, nor knew the meaning of Don Quixote's
wind-mill fight, until I had witnessed the vaporings of
this blustering sect. My allusion is by no means meant to
embrace all who wore cockades, but only those of them who
declined without excuse, participating in any department of
a service they had exercised such an active agency in origi-
nating. Those men who, (like Longstreet's character,) were
"jest aseein how they could a fout." But some, even of the
class referred to, deserve to be excused from censure. *They*

*The Author has received a statement of the interesting incidents that
occurred during this absence, but they came too late to be arranged and
methodized for insertion in the present edition. [Warren's note.]

wore *cockades*, and were minute men, but theirs were not fighting cockades, they were—judging by the language their conduct has spoken—"ready at a minute's warning" to shove other people into the scrape. Others, again, of the cockade fraternity, were furiously bellicose at the beginning, but learning that an ungrateful country actually declined to furnish them with conveyances to ride in, umbrellas to keep the sun off and furloughs to cut the gentleman whenever asked for, indignantly refused to blister their tender feet and scorch their delicate faces in behalf of any such unfeeling and improvident government, and who blames them? But they wont wear any more cockades. No indeed, you couldn't put a bridle on their heads strong enough to lead them up to one again. Well, as I was saying, Fishback came home wearing a grand looking cockade, and immediately connected himself with one of the companies then being made up in this county, and in the organization run for third lieutenant and was defeated.

Claiming that the men of the company had mistreated him, he soon after dissolved his connection with them and moving his mother off, left us, I hope, forever. A Captain's uniform the ladies had been preparing with great care and no little expense, disappeared about the time of his departure, but whether it was taken by him is not positively known. He went from this to Wilcox county, and rumor says, committed some offence for which the civil authorities were about to handle him, when he *refugeed* to your regiment, then about to be mustered into service at Griffin. I infer from your letter that he has behaved better, or at least, more cautiously in the Old Dominion, than he did here. You will be satisfied eventually, that he is the very soul of treachery, dissimulation and villainy.

I doubt whether he was sick at all when you left him by the roadside, and I give it as my opinion, that, if you will administer a dose of ipecac to the Richmond prisons, some one of them will puke him up. But you needn't hunt him, he cant be made to fight or do any other duty, and the most rigid discipline will never restrain him from exercising his proficiency in the art of theft, lying and general rascality. Finally, Capt., old fell, manage this war the best you can, and end it as quick as possible, for I am terribly afraid if it lasts long they'll jerk me into the row. That kind of life wouldn't suit me. It *spiles* my temper to be mixed up with anything, either operose or bellicose. My nest is warm and comfortable, and I must needs lie in it. I love my native land, but I love it like a brother, (as the girls tell a fellow when they reject him,) not with the romantic martial attachment of a knight or champion. Read this letter to my "inseparable associate," and give him my comps, and believe me to be, with great, &c., &c., &c.,

Your very &c., &c., &c.,
J. RUFUS BATES.

The information contained in this letter, though not (as Captain Smith thought) accompanied with any symptoms of infallibility, was so confirmed by the disclosures contained in Fishback's letter and suspicions he himself had begun to indulge, that the Capt., as has already been stated, felt a perfect indifference on the subject of his incarceration. Now reader, the evidence in favor of Smith, is closed, and the whole case submitted. Whether he was "guilty or not guilty" of unjustifiable negligence in leaving our hero thus hampered "by outrageous fortune," must rest with your decision, unless posterity shall see fit to disturb the verdict you render, by exercising appellate jurisdiction.

CHAPTER IV

In which our Hero gets squirted out of his Richmond board-
ing-house and tumbles, with dignity, into the arms of his
beloved Capt.,—Feels, at first, the influence of a frigid
shoulder, but having out-lived that, at length ascends to
a position of great grandeur,—Displays the first order of
financiering talents, together with a strong mixture of
tact and prescience,—Gets acquainted with his future
biographer, and produces favorable impressions on the
mind of that gentleman:

The two armies now hung threateningly around the Confederate Capitol, the big event was unquestionably close at
hand, and every nerve was strained to get all convenient
absentees to the post of duty. Prisons and Hospitals were
disgorged of their surplus contents, and many a cozy bunk
left riderless and

> "Alone,
> Like Adam's recollection of his fall."

This process restored the unfortunate Fishback to his command. The reception he met with was far from being such
an one as he had expected. Capt. Smith was making out a
pay-roll when he came up, and merely stopping to tell him
howdye, went on with his writing. Not a question was asked
by any officer of the company upon the subject of his late
imprisonment, the circumstances of his release, or indeed
any of the scenes through which he had passed during his
long and *puny* absence. Our hero felt keenly the influence
of the "cold shoulder" turned to him, but didn't let on.

It was not long before Jenkins, a member of the company,
informed him that Rufus Bates had written the Capt. a letter
paying some very bulky left-handed compliments to his
integrity and fighting qualities. Our hero was a man of policy.
Although, from the frequency of his scrapes, he had, of
necessity, often been detected, yet, his judgment was, nevertheless, good, his plans always well formed and his instincts

unerring. He, therefore, received this unwelcome intelligence with perfect composure. Had he laughed at it, his levity might have been regarded as an effort to cloak suspicion and smother remorseful feelings; on the contrary, had he grown furious in the manifestations of his anger, would have been read, the writhings of a guilty victim under the tortures of the lash. Our sagacious hero pursued neither course. "Ah, nobody haint got no confidence in Rufe Bates" said he, "nothin he sez cuddent pester me. Them biskits is a bakin a *leetle* too fast. Je-e-e-e-- rusalum! ef yonder aint Dick Ellis a fetchin in a hole peck o' taters. Wonder what creek he ketcht em outen?"

"Bill," resumed Jenkins, "I believe the Capt. thinks every word Rufus Bates said is true."

"Shucks, no he don't, I tell you nobody don't never bleve nary word Rufe Bates sez, he's drunk rite now,—don't put no more wood on the fire, my biskits'l burn into ashes afore they git warm through—how I do sweat."

"The Capt. didn't tell any of us a word about the letter, but as my tent fly was stretched close to his I heard him reading it to the Lieutenants, and when he got through they all made some pretty harsh remarks about you."

"You was jest a dreamin, Jinks. Capn noze I'm all chuck. These biskits is like old Joner, they'er a gwine into the belly uv a whale."

At this moment the sound of battle was heard far up the Chickahominy on the opposite side. Drums were beat, roll-calls gone through with, and every body ordered to be ready to move out. Late in the evening the regiment to which Capt. Smith belonged was carried down the river and placed in position. The Capt. now began to watch our hero closely, and to use towards him none but the most curt and positive language. But no evidence of official disfavor seemed to reach the mind of the imperturbable Fishback. He had mapped out his future policy and intended unfalteringly to pursue it. The regiment was hurried from one point to another without being engaged *in actubelli*, until the 1st of July, at which time it mingled with the countless multitudes that swarmed along the slopes of Malvern Hill. Our hero was with his command, and exhibited remarkable coolness and self-possession. "Jest look, Capn," said he, as they halted under a furious fire, "jest look how them ar gun bote bullits tars up the ground, they haint got no respect fur the rites o' property. See how that thing whackt off that simmon tree; now hits swindled sum possum outen a good bate uv simmons. Jeminy how them blu whislers whissels, they must a tuck lessons in a whislin skule. Wonder why they dont let us charge sumthin ur go sumwhar, this sun shines hot enuf to scorch minners, hits ekle to a firy furnish." Presently they were ordered around to the left, when a spirited engagement took place, in which our hero behaved with an intrepidity that attracted the attention and elicited the commendations of all who saw him, and at the close of the action came off the field *sans vulnere*.

Young Bates was now set down as an idle, profligate, and worthless slanderer, and Fishback was as high above par with the Captain as he had recently been below.

It was during the calm that succeeded these battles, when the "Company Qs" were organized into a society, (the by-laws, words, signs and grips of which will be found in the appendix to this volume,) our hero being considered the most suitable man to perform the important and responsible duties of first president, was elected with but little difficulty to that position. He had occupied this exalted station but two weeks when, having been caught in the violation of section 6, he was impeached and expelled from the brotherhood. Fishback being, therefore, entirely unconnected with this secret institution, it will be alluded to no more in the body of this work.

Knowing the Captain was fond of flattery, our hero, on his sudden restoration to power, began to administer to that officer large and frequent draughts of this cheap and innoxious but very intoxicating beverage. The warm hearted Captain honestly reciprocating these manisfestations of good opinion, likewise pampered his lovely Billy with the pap of praise.

Although writers on philosophy have (by a most blunder-ing oversight) neglected to mention the "attraction of tit-illation," yet, it is certainly the strongest of all attractions. You have noticed, reader, that if you can only manage to get close enough to a hog, (wild though he may be) to tickle him good on the belly with a stick, he will lie down, close his eyes and surrender without a solitary article of capitulation. It is thus with human beings, tickle them—don't hurt them—but tickle them good with flattery, and if they are sufficiently approachable for you to rub it on well, they will close their eyes to whatever sinister purposes you may have in view, and resign themselves unconditionally to your control. This is the result, not of psychological legerdemain, but of right reason. The person who considers you a man of intellect and a high-toned gentleman, shows himself to be a judge of such matters, a man of discernment, and inasmuch as he likes you, it is quite evident that he appreciates and esteems those traits, and must, therefore, labor to possess them. Such a man undoubtedly merits your love, of course he does.

Under the influence of this attraction our hero and his Captain grew to each other like Damon and Pythias. The one became the other's shadow.

It was not long before they obtained passes and went to town together. On their arrival, Fishback generously purchased a bottle of whiskey, with which they twain began to fire up. One drink invited another, which invited a third, until our hero found it necessary to engage a bed for the Captain who was no longer able to keep his feet. He was accordingly undressed and put to bed, after having been again well drenched by his thoughtful and considerate warden.

No sooner were Capt. Smith's eyes closed in the deep sleep of drunkenness than Fishback commenced making an inventory of his pocket-book which was found to contain nine hundred and sixty dollars. Taking out five hundred, he carefully replaced the balance, donned the Captain's uniform and sallied into the street. Arriving in front of Welch's store, he suddenly put on a drunken look, pulled his hat over his face, and staggered in. "Keep this fur me twell I git sober" said he, reaching the pocket-book to a man who stood behind the counter.

"What name, Captain?" asked the other, as he took the book in his hand.

"John Smith, Captain Company ——, —— Georgia Regiment," replied the stupid looking Fishback, as he reeled away, disregarding the polite "very well sir," that followed him. About two o'clock, P. M., Captain Smith awoke and found his intimate sitting by the bed patiently fanning the flies off of him. "Here Cap'n" said he, "take a drink, and here's sum vittels I had fetcht up for you, eat quick and less leve, our time's out." The Captain felt very little like taking anything internally; but knowing it would be of advantage to his health and an accommodation to Billy, he indulged in a swig, ate a hasty snack, and they left for camps. Just as they were getting to the regiment, a boy came along with pies for sale.

"This way my little man," said the Captain, reaching a hand into his pocket, when lo! his money was gone. "Billy" said he, at the same time examining and re-examining every part of his clothes, "*do you know* what I did with my pocket-book?"

"No Capn," replied Fishback. "I tried to git you to give it to me to keep, but you cust me and sed you wooddent. Sed you'd got a letter about me, and you was a gwine to giv it to a onist man to keep. Treckly you cum and cust me agin and sed you'd dun give it to a feller as woodn't steal it." This statement bore unmistakeable marks of truth on its face. Fishback could not possibly have heard of the Bates letter, unless he had been thus informed, since not a member of the company was allowed to know one word about it. Smith therefore went to every friend he remembered to have seen in town, and inquired, but in vain, after the missing treasure. A faint suspicion was now harbored in his mind that although he had undoubtedly used the offensive language referred to by Fishback, yet Fishback, on his part, might, nevertheless, have purloined the money. So, creeping to that gentleman's tent at a late hour of the night, he gave his pockets a thorough searching and found them to contain only fifty cents in Confederate money.

"Now" thought he, "the poor fellow has spent his last dollar treating me—has watched over and attended to me like a brother, and here I have suspected him of theft at a time when he is sleeping in the security of conscious innocence, and repaid his kindness with the worst ingratitude. He is an honest man and a clever fellow, and I'll not be imposed upon by foul suspicion or brainless scribblers any more." Fishback, who meanwhile lay snoring and occasionally champing, was nevertheless, wide wake, and congratulating himself upon the manner in which this looked-for search would vindicate his honesty and innocence. Next day, at his recommendation, the Captain sent an advertisement to the Richmond *Dispatch*, asking to be informed through the mail with whom the pocket-book had been deposited. Mr. Welch replied promptly that it was left with him, and that he held it and contents subject to Capt Smith's order. I have no room here to insert the particulars of the difficulty that occurred between the Captain and Welch when the former called in. He of course insisted that the money was five hundred dollars short of the right amount. While Welch madly denied that the pocket-book had been opened since he (Smith) left it there. The one was advised to stay sober in future and take care of his own money, the other was instructed in the propriety of turning himself into an honest man. Altercation was followed by threats, until the city police interfered and quelled the disturbance. This circumstance necessarily had a fattening effect upon our hero's reputation. Indeed, it brought him on the very front pew in the synagogue of Smith's affections.

"Told you" he remarked, "you'd gone and give it to sumbody. I wish I'd a jest tuck it any how, but you wus rite, you thought maby Ide teck some on it. But I aint a thinkin no ways hard uv you, fokes had bin a tellin lies on me. No, no, Capn you thought you'd give it to a onester man, and I dont think no less uv you. Swar pine blank I wooddent swap my Capn fur all Capns in the nunited world. I'me willin to wait and let you cuss me when you git drunk, and think I'me a rogue, fur I know you'l larn me atter a while."

This last observation had one meaning in the mind of Fishback and was meant to convey another to that of the Captain, who replied: "Yes Billy, I have done you great and gross injustice, which no one could regret more than I do. You have certainly proved yourself an honest man and a brave and faithful soldier. I was misled by Rufus Bates, a young man whose name I had heard you mention kindly. He wrote me a drunken sort of a letter containing a great many false accusations against you. I am astonished that I ever placed the least confidence in one word it contained."

"*Rufe Bates*? why he's a drunkard. I whipt *him* like a dog. They like to sent Mister Rufe to the Milledgeville for burnin up a skule house."

"Why he wrote that you burned the school house, and were so strongly suspected that you had to flee the country."

"*He did?*" inquired Fishback, with the greatest apparent surprise and indignation, "blasted ef I didn't give him ninety dollars to git off with when his own daddy turned agin him."

"Yes, and he accused you of stealing ninety dollars from his father."

"*Who! me?* Darned ef I didn't let him have it outen my own hand,—glad now the teacher whipt him bout that pitcher on the dore ef sum uv them little gals did make it."

"Well, Billy, I see the scoundrel has substituted your name in every instance, where his own belonged. *I* am satisfied, and not only satisfied, but gratified with your character. So, since this conversation is disagreeable let's drop the subject."

About the time spoken of, the army broke up camps and moved off in the direction of Manassas. It was while they halted near Gordonsville, that the writer of these pages formed the acquaintance of that distinguished individual whose biographer he was destined in future to become.

Tired of camp fare, I one evening obtained permission to go anywhere within three miles of my company quarters and get supper at a house. The citizens in that neighborhood had been treated so badly by straggling soldiers, that I (not having the recommendation of a prepossessing personal appearance) found it no easy matter to get my name in the pot anywhere. Having been turned off at a good many places I had strolled nearly to my limit, when I came across a soldier sitting on a log by the road-side industriously devouring a piece of chicken and some bread. "Where" I asked, "did you happen to that luck, my friend?"

"Up yander," said he pointing to a neighboring house, and speaking through his teeth, which were clenched on a piece of chicken he was resolutely laboring to pull loose from the bone, "taint fur, spozen you go up and try yore luck."

"Is there any chance for me to get supper there?"

"Nary chance; the way I cum to git in, as I went up I met a soger cumin away. Mister, sez he, you'd jist as well go back; sez he, thars no more showin fur you at that ar house nor thar is fur a bob-tailed cow in fly time, sez he. I axed him *why.* Kase, sez he, a hole raft uv thar kin's jest cum up in a carrage to ete em out, sez he, and more'n that, sez he, the ginral's put a guard round the house, sez he. Well, on I went, when I got to the guard, halt, sez he, hey, sez I furgot me already? Don't you rickollect me a cummin in that ar carrage, sez I. Oh yes, sez he, cum in, and he looked mity shamed about haltin uv me. Well, I went in the house and I told the old umun, I did, sez I, I'me a new guard that's jest been sent out, sez I, to releve one uv the old uns that's cumplainin, sez I, and I'me nately sick I'me so hongry, haint tasted vittels sense yistiddy mornin, sez I. The old umun she pitted me mitely and she went to the cubburd, she did, and she got me this and I tuck hit and gerkt up a good pockit nife I seed a lyin luce and cum off. Mister, got enny good chaw-in tubacker?" I gave him a chew of the desired weed, smiled at his drollery, and passed on. A little after dusk—the most favorable time for a homely soldier to find accommodations in a strange country—I came to the residence of Mr. Hen-derson, and applied for supper. The good lady informed me that her husband was from home and she did not feel disposed to entertain strangers in his absence, but having satisfied her that I would settle my bill and otherwise behave in a respect-ful and becoming manner, she at length invited me in. Present-ly, the youth with whom I had conversed on the road, and who, I assure you, dear reader, was none other than the veritable Fishback, came up. "Overtuck you agin, old Miss kin I git supper here" said he, speaking to both of us in the same breath and without regard to punctuation. She replied affirmatively, but with evident reluctance. The children, con-sisting of George, a boy about fifteen; Lula, a girl thirteen, and several snug little specimens of the trundle-bed tribe, for some purpose or other, now began to arrange themselves around the fire.

The whole of this little group manifested such dignity and good breeding, as quite charmed and captivated me. Lula and George, as subsequent developements proved, pos-sessed ticklish souls, and it was right they should. All nature smiles upon the young; let them reflect the smile, let them laugh away the bright, happy morning of existence, for with its evening come sorrow and tears. Fishback was, on this occasion, by no means economical of his homespun observa-tions, nor shy about exhibiting those clumsy manners that constituted the sweetening in the cup of his heroism. The young people managed, by dint of rigid self-control, apparently not to notice anything unusual for some time. At length Mrs. Henderson got to talking on her favorite subject —the virtues and merits of the Baptist Church—in which I (being a Baptist myself) participated with some zest. Antinomianism, landmarkism and all other isms were being paraded before us, and reviewed in their order.

"The doctrines of John Agricola," said she, "may be branded with the stigma of 'heresies,' but I honestly believe that with very slight modification they contain the"—here our hero gaping, laying his head back, stretching both arms to full length and showing no regard whatever to the conversation going on, remarked,—"my fokes is all baptises and I wisht I was at a big baptis metin rite now. My daddy wus one uv the bess baptis preachers in Georgy. You could a hearn him preach mor'n a mile." George and Lula now exploded upsetting the gravity of all present, (our good natured hero not excepted.) He didn't, however, understand the object of the laugh, and didn't care to show his ignorance by asking.

At length we were summoned into the supper-room, a neat, little, closely constructed apartment with new ceiling and no window or other outlet than the one at which we entered.

The table was *ornamented* with coffee, biscuit, fried chicken and ham; tripe, fried in batter, plum preserves, &c., &c., all prepared in the most palatable style. Staying his fork into a piece of the tripe—which, prepared as it had been—of course looked to the *naked* eye, like a flour fixing, he brought it to his teeth, gave a pull and then laying it quietly on his plate, looked me full in the face, and with an air of impressive seriousness remarked: "Well, sir, this here flitter's got a rag in it." The whole table went into convulsions, Fishback this time excepted. Mrs. Henderson spilt a cup of coffee she was handing, George swallowed a fourth of a biscuit the wrong way, Lula emptied the contents of her plate, and I—I went into spasms. Order was at length restored and the eating went on, our hero evidently manifesting, by his solemnity, the premonitory symptoms of a growl. Directly the preserves were handed round, and having helped himself he began to champ them in regular hog and hickory-nut fashion. As he pressed one of the slick seeds between his teeth trying to suck the juice out, it popped from his mouth with great velocity and passing between the heads of Lula and George, which were close together, struck the new ceiling of that close room with such a crash as made even Fishback jump. George and Lula both dodged, and the former having requested our hero to "be particular which way he pointed the muzzle of that gun especially when it was loaded," we need hardly state the table again shook under the influence of a general laugh. Mrs. Henderson scolded the children for being so foolish, but was compelled by the force of circumstances, to set them a *laughable* example of the folly she condemned.

Supper being over, Fishback and I paid our bills and set out for camps. I with a light heart, and he—with a good supply of rations he had managed to smuggle during the excitement.

"Now didn't that young buck blate," said he, as we passed through the gate. "Wonder what battle he lost his manners in? and that young umun, how she did cackle and squeal. Well, they aint mor'n made expenses outen me, for I give em bad munny fur my sepper, and here's what's left, (displaying the provisions he had stolen.) The old umun lemme have four dollars and a haff and my sepper for a five on the Munro Rale rode bank. Wonder ef that'l be funny when she finds it out. Maby hit'l make em all laff on the tother side uv thar dod-rotted mouth yit. No sich as that aint a hurtin o' none o' my feelins. What's that you got on, Mister?"

"It's a satchel," said I, "in which I carry several valuable keep sakes, and a number of curiosities I have picked up."

"By jings, hit's a nise trick, pull it off and lemme look at it, think I'll have me one made jest like it only with a *leetle* bigger flap." I, of course, handed him the satchel, and he walked along making many extravagant remarks about it, until at length he saw me bending down to get a drink out of a spring near the road, when satchel, contents, Fishback and all mysteriously disappeared.

Next morning I went in search of him to the regiment and company of which he had told me he was a member, but the Orderly Sergeant stated that no such name had ever been entered on his muster-roll. The satchel contained, among other things, a Testament, the gift of my beloved Pastor, and "March's Life of Webster," presented by Linda the morning I left home, with a special charge to "preserve it as I valued her love." I felt no disposition to give up such sacred souvenirs, and was walking slowly back to my quarters, trying to think up some plan by which the rogue might be tracked to his lurking place, when suddenly I stumbled upon the regiment, company and person of William Fishback himself, and demanded restoration of the stolen goods. "You'r a start nateral fool; I never seed yore things, and don't no nuthin about em," was his mild and amiable reply.

"Look here now," said I, "you know you took the things; just give me the contents of the satchel, you've got no use in the world for them, and you may have the satchel itself."

"D-o-o-o-o what? I haint had none uv yore things, and you'd better leve here" he replied, rising up in a very rebuking, not to say threatening manner.

"Well," said I, "I'll see your Captain about it."

"And so'll I" he remarked, as we both approached that officer's tent. "Capn here's that same cussed Rufe Bates persecutin me agin, and accusin me uv stealin."

In vain did I deny that I was Rufe Bates, or that I had ever heard that name before. My sentences were all broken off in the middle by the emphatic order "shut your mouth" accompanied with a tornado of ugly words. To be brief, a multitude of curses and kicks from the Captain and a summary ejection from his quarters, with a positive injunction, "never to show my shapes around him any more," were all the restitution I received of my stolen possessions. As I was hastily and with great pain and no little mortification making my way off Fishback called to me: "See here Rufe, old fel, cum to see us agin, and ef you can't cum, rite us anuther one uv them ar letters, we'll be mity proud to here frum you."

Reader, you have now, an account of the manner in which my acquaintance with Fishback commenced. Would you like to receive a similar introduction? Do you yearn to shelter yourself beneath the shadow of so towering a personage? Ponder the matter seriously while I prepare for your perusal another and a most important chapter of his eventful history.

CHAPTER V

In which our Hero once more abandons the tedium of camp-life,—Gets a capital joke on Dick Ellis,—Meets up with a disagreeable gentleman at the residence of Mrs. Lane, —Is so much displeased with the gentleman's manners, that he leaves,—In fact vamoses,—Gets to Major Graves', —Becomes a Hero, indeed, and finally sees his star pass from its zenith to the nadir, in less than a twinkling.

A day or two after the occurrences related in the last chapter, Lee's army moved off in the direction of Culpepper, and our hero having previously hired an adept in the writing business, to prepare some papers for him, started back in the direction from which he had traveled in the commencement of his public career. Don't understand me as saying that he went off on those vulgar vehicles, his feet.

While official chargers were in every part of the army, he would have been untrue to the first law of nature had he condescended to take the people's line. On the contrary, when it was announced over night that the forces would move out by day-light next morning, he and Dick Ellis retired to a log and set their wits in motion to work out some plan by which they might both mount themselves and effect their escape without apprehension. Ellis had a brother in the Federal service at Yorktown, and thither he determined to go. Fishback consented to bear him company, yet had no idea of doing so. It was not a part of his programme thus to sleep off the golden dreams that were flitting before his mind. But no common mortal like Ellis was permitted to peep into the sanctum of his intentions. Well, each took an oath never to reveal a word that passed between them in this conference, and then set to planning. Major Holmes had one of the finest horses in the army. Fishback knowing that the better the animal, the greater would be the efforts to re-secure him, kindly proffered to aid in stealing *that horse* for Dick. Dick was to leave about midnight in the direction of West Point. Two hours afterwards Fishback would go to the Major, inform him of the theft, state that he had tried to stop the rogue but being afoot could not, that if he only had a horse he would certainly catch him, for he knew precisely which way he had gone. If the Major refused to send him he was to give the wrong directions to whoever was sent in pursuit, and steal off the best he could; if, however, as was not doubted, he would mount Fishback and start him, they could get together and jog along as leisurely as they desired, having no one at all on their trail. About four miles from camp, and along a dim, unfrequented thorough-way, Dick was to wait until our hero came up, when they were to make for the Federal lines at Bottom's bridge.

Sure enough, about two o'clock, A. M., Fishback rushed into the Major's tent breathless with running and excitement, and began to shake him. "Majer, Majer,!"

"What the dickens do you want?"

"Somebody's stold yore hoss, and rid him off. I met him when I wus a cummin off uv guard jest now and tried to stop him; he's gwine a toards Beaver Dam. I know jest whar he's gone."

"Well, well, well, I'm sorry for that. Fishback, can't you go after him for me? Wake up Adjutant, I want to borrow your horse to send after mine; some scoundrel's stolen him. Fishback, Capt. Smith thinks you can do anything you put your hand to: catch my horse and I'll entertain the same opinion, besides giving you a round hundred dollars; and here, take my pistol and kill the villain wherever you lay eyes on him." This pistol business presented a new idea to the mind of our hero, who thereupon suggested that as there were several roads, it would be well enough to send some one with him. Fishback and Jack Wilcox were, therefore, properly instructed, "armed to the teeth," in the stirrups and off at a lope in less time than a stuttering man could have told about it. "Don't come back without my horse," bawled out Holmes, as the riders disappeared.

They had not gone far before Fishback came to a sudden halt, and bending as far down as possible, looked intently on the ground. "Here's hosses tracks" said he, "this rode's mity dim, but goze into tother one about five miles from here, and *hit* cuts off a little. I gess he's gone it. You go thru and I'll go round. The Major's told us to kill him when we cetch him, and we're ableeged to do it. I dont luv to kill fokes, you'r a heap dangerouser man than I am, you take *hit*."

This well seasoned morsel of flattery had the desired effect. "Yes" observed Jack, "I'll follow him, and if he gets overhauled by me his infernal skull will leak shucks after this."

Thus they parted, the one congratulating himself that "dead men tell no tales" and the other burning with a murderous revengeful spirit.

From the difficulty of inquiring the direction to the place he was aiming for, Fishback lost considerable distance and took a number of wrong roads.

About noon of the second day after his departure, he was traveling slowly along, his head down and mind buried in deep study. "Yes, I'll fool him like I did about the Rufe Bates letter and the pocket-book and all, taint no trouble to fool him. I'll jest tell how sum feller tride to teck my hoss away, and we fout, and how he nockt me down and crippled me so I never walkt a step in two munths, and then jumpt a straddle o' my hoss and gallopt off. Never shall furgit the Majer's last words 'don't cum back thout my hoss,' nur I haint. Capn Smith's a thinkin o' me rite now, he luves his 'brave, onest Billy.' Dick Ellis aint a guine to pester about tellin nothin. That fool Jack's dun turned him over to the tender mersez uv the carron croze. That's a good joke I've got on Dick, maniged to git his branes shot out thout my tellin a word." He was just raising his head to enjoy a good laugh over this pleasant and amusing little incident, when he found himself immediately before the cabin of his old friend Mrs. Lane. It was several miles to the next house; he felt hungry and weary. The prospects of being identified, (considering the number of soldiers who had passed at various times, and the situation of the "widder," during his former visit,) were very small, and then too, the cheering reflection that "widders don't hurt," constituted argument sufficient to control his decision on the question whether he would stop for dinner. But first, our wary Fishback asked a child he saw playing in the yard, whether its "mammy" had married again, and having received a negative reply, threw his bridle over the gate-post, walked in, engaged dinner, dashed himself into a seat and was again lost in the delightful revery his arrival had so abruptly interrupted.

Directly, a grim, surly looking man, wearing heavy, black, whiskers, badly pock-marked, and carrying the remains of a deep scar in his right cheek, passed through the room, giving our hero, as *he* thought, a very indelicate stare. This circumstance not only broke up his meditations but opened the eyes of Fishback to a number of remarkable truths. The stranger passed into the apartment he had slept in; he saw the old shanty had given place to a neat shed-room opening in the rear upon a snug row of negro houses. His quick perception immediately convinced him that "the child had fooled him on purpose, and the widder *wus marred* again."

We will here explain for the benefit of the reader, that Mrs. Lane *never did* suspect our hero of having stolen Bones or the blankets. The events of the morning were of such a character that that antiquated animal had not been thought of until near noon, when he was found quietly occupying the lot to which he had returned. It is true, he had on a saddle and bridle and the gate was open, but Col. Lane merely set him to rights, and (his mind being engrossed with other matters) did not think to mention it. The missing blankets were charged to the roguery of an innocent man, and one of the children *distinctly* saw the soldier, (meaning Fishback) leave about day-light, and "directly after papa came home." Mrs. Lane was a little afraid her neglect had wounded his feelings. But after all, on that happy morning there was no room in the minds of the Lane family to be occupied by a strange soldier, so even our hero was cared for, and thought of no more. Col. Lane regained a portion of his property, left his wife comfortable and went back to the army.

On the day of Fishback's return, a neighbor had agreed with Mrs. Lane, to call over at noon and superintend the killing of a beef, in which they were both interested. That neighbor was the man whose presence so unmercifully disquieted our hero. After some stirring round he and Mrs. Lane took a stand near the room door, (the former holding in his hand a huge butcher-knife) and began to converse in an under tone, each eveing him in a way he fancied exhibited no great sociability. The children too, stared at him in a most uncomfortable manner. He wanted to leave but was afraid the butcher knife would be inserted into his corpus the moment he made the break. At this juncture he looked out and saw his horse's tail disappearing behind the lot gate, and shrunk back trembling, sweating and rolling his eyes as the "brave Billy" had never done before. Occasionally his ear would catch disjointed fragments of sentences uttered by the sotto voce talkers such as the "skin him," "butcher him," &c., either of which were sufficiently diaphoretic in its effects to put him into what the doctors call "a fine perspiration." But his suspense, although it seemed an age, did not last long. Presently the man in the whiskers remarked—as our hero thought—in an alarmingly vehement manner, "I'll get the gun and shoot him now," accompanying the words with a brisk movement into the room he was occupying. Fishback didn't stay to the shooting. Having sprung out at the door, he wrenched open the gate and ran for dear life, allowing his horse to eat "at will" and leaving the astonished family a striking example of the uncertainty of human nature and mortal legs.

Having measured the distance of five miles with such rapidity as to quite exhaust his wind and strength, Fishback crept into a thicket and sat down to rest.

"Well, now haint I done it" said he. "Lost my hoss and all my clene close by jest not havin no sense. Mite a node it wont safe to stop thar, but I wus so hungry and wornt afeard o' wimmin, and jest nately wonted to see how the widder wus a gittin on starvin. That husband o' hern's a everlastin fool, jest a gwine to shute a feller thout saying peze to him. Them vittles they was a fetchin in did smell monstrous invitin. Ding it all I'me a hongry, hit's raal mean not to feed a feller whats fitin fur the country. When *I fit* I fit fur the country so's to make the country fit fur me, and this is the ways its all turned out. Well reckon I'll git sum more cloze by then I retch old man Graveses and these passes I've got and them'l last me twell more cums in. Hit's a most too clost by to be a pickin up a nuther hoss."

Without any further adventure of a noteworthy character, our hero marched on, and late in the evening of the next day, reached Major Graves'.

He reminded the family of having called there before, but so many soldiers had stopped in passing that the Major could not recollect him until he referred to the then recent death of his father and the unsettled condition of the estate. "Oh yes, sir, yes sir," said he, "I remember you well, you are often pleasantly mentioned in my family. It is so strange my old eyes would not at first assist me to identify you. Well, sir, to what fortunate circumstance are we indebted for your present visit? Have a seat, sir, let me take your hat."

"Mammy was a lyin at the pint uv death and sent me word to cum home and stay with her twell she died. So atter the fites round Richmond, I got a discharge and jest as I was a gwine to start home I got a letter sayin she was dead"—here he shook his head mournfully and winked fast, as if to dissipate an intruding tear. "So I bought me a hoss and started back to the army—my hoss lay down and died yisteddy. I'm a gwine to the front, hit's the only place for me, a poor olphin, to go to—must start mighty soon in the mornin." One of the young ladies suggested, that as he was evidently very much wearied by hard marching, and the weather so oppressively warm, it would perhaps be an economy of time in the long run, for him to stop over a day or two. "Ah gal" said he, speaking very seriously, "I'd like to stay monstrous well, but my bleedin country axes me with tears in hit's eyes, to come up to the scratch, and thar I mean to come, so help me Jerediah Moss."

This stirring and patriotic speech was rewarded by an immediate invitation to supper. Soon after eating, he plead weariness and retired; not, however, until he had given Miss "Calline" several ingenuous manifestations of tender feeling, which only served as a source of amusement to her.

Next morning, Fishback was a bed-ridden, and badly tortured victim of rheumatism. Major Graves came in to see him, and prescribed a perfect diarrhoea of remedies. "No use projickin with medicines when I'm this way," said . Fishback,—"hit don't do narry speck o' good, this nasty, stinkin rumatism's allers a pesterin me, and the Doctor says pills and draps makes it a sight wuss. Here Major, retch thar in my pocket and git my pocket-book, and carry hit to Miss Graves, and tell her to keep it for me twel I git well, and not to let nobody open it; hit's a holdin secrets I'd hate mighty bad for *any boddy* to find out."

The wise Fishback had placed a proper estimate on female curiosity. He knew that after his injunction was announced the "gals" would "move heaven and earth" to pry into the mysteries of the pocket-book. Sure enough, they watched where their mother deposited it and as soon as her back was turned, stole it out, went to their own room, locked the door and began to hunt the *forbidden* secrets. The pocket-book was found to contain eleven hundred and thirty dollars, a discharge "granted William Fishback to return home and superintend the large agricultural interests of his mother, Mrs. Prissy Fishback," and also a letter, which read as follows:

ISABELLA, July 2d, 1862.

MR. WILLIAM FISHBACK,

Honored Sir:—It becomes my melancholy duty to inform you that your excellent mother is now no more. She died on the night of the 22nd ult., from congestion of the brain, superinduced, as you know, by a combination of pre-existing diseases.

During her last illness she spoke of you often, and expressed great anxiety to see you. I know you have been long anticipating this sad event, but it will, of course, cast a gloom over your feelings, as it has over those of all her friends. I never knew a woman so universally beloved, nor one so unceasingly kind, attentive and charitable to the suffering and needy. But, waiving these sorrowful suggestions, I must give you some information with reference to the situation of the estate, which now belongs solely to you. As there were a good many outstanding matters that required immediate attention, I have, at the urgent solicitation of your overseer, taken out temporary letters of administration. I sincerely hope you will be allowed to come home and manage the business yourself. I have too many matters of my own to look after, just now, to be well able to assume such additional and weighty responsibilities with justice to myself. I had the appraisement yesterday, your negroes and real estate were valued at $98,503 89; Bank and railroad stock $16,336 04; ready money and Sterling Exchange, $16,944 00; notes and accounts $18,620 00; making a total of $148,404 93. The whole of this estimate made on a gold and silver basis. The stock and household and kitchen furniture, including the piano and the two sofas, were not embraced in this appraisement, as it was understood that they belonged to you individually. There were a good many other things left out which it was not thought necessary to appraise. I understand the indebtedness of the estate is less than $1,800. The present crop promises well, and will pay that amount easily. The overseer informs me that the prospect was never so good at this season of the year, before.

Capt. Anderson, our representative, was killed, (as you know) at Port Republic, and there is great anxiety among the citizens generally, for you to be elected to fill his vacancy. There is a flying report in circulation here that you have been consulted on the subject and declined the candidacy. I hope and believe this rumor is without foundation, since it is certainly true that you are the only man in Worth county who could be elected without opposition. This is peculiarly a time when everything like political feeling and election excitement should be avoided, and as it is in your power so easily to harmonize all conflicting elements by representing Worth, I earnestly hope you will not refuse to do so. And in addition to this, you won't consider it flattery in an old and intimate friend, and one who you know appreciates you, to say that your force of character, your patriotic energy and earnestness in behalf of the cause, your strength and vigor of mind, and above all, the unspotted purity of your whole life, eminently entitle you to a seat in the Georgia Legislature, and give earnest of the useful manner in which you will honor and dignify the position. Under all the circumstances, I really think, my dear sir, that you can serve the country more effectually in that way than any other.

Hoping soon to receive an answer giving me permission to place your name before the citizens of Worth,

I am, respected sir, with much esteem,

Your very sincere friend,
JOEL T. OLIVER

Although, as we have stated, this inspection was conducted in secret session and with closed doors, yet no sooner was it completed than the whole group rushed into the presence of the old people and made a full revelation of all their discoveries. This, of course, resulted in a long family chat. The

Major concluded that "although Fishback was illiterate, *he* had not been mistaken in regarding the young man as a solid, reliable, high-toned youth, and one that would work his passage through life."

Mrs. Graves thought "he was yet quite young and could undoubtedly get the rust rubbed off by mixing a little with the world, representing his county in a few sessions of the Georgia Legislature, and marrying an educated girl." In making this last remark, her eyes fell, by the purest accident, on Caroline, who blushed deeply and replied that she "didn't believe Mr. Fishback wanted to marry anybody."

"Wife," remarked the Major, "I think he is rather pleased with Caroline. Go, my daughter, and comb your hair and button on your collar; it's eleven o'clock, and he thinks he'll be well enough to come down to dinner. Children, be particular, and don't let him have any reason to suspect that you have opened his pocket-book. What laudable modesty, to thus shrink from an examination of papers that stamp his character with the impress of Honor! Go Caroline, and fix yourself up."

"Ma" said little Ellen, "when sis Carline and Mr. Fishback marries mayn't I go to Georgy wid em and be dare baby?" This observation was followed by a loud laugh on the part of the young ladies, a scolding from Mrs. Graves and an adjournment of the convention.

The Misses Graves were now wholly forgetful of the fact that they had ever giggled at the comical chat and gawkish manners of our hero. There was nothing gawkish or comical about him. *He was such a nice gentleman,—so original and unaffected—deported himself in such an artless and independent manner, and might be so appropriately said to draw the language in which he conversed, from Nature's pure, unwrought well-spring.* When dinner was announced, Fishback, supported by the Major, hobbled down stairs, and made his way to the table.

By one of those thoroughly intentional *accidents* that are "fixed aforehand," his chair and that of Miss Caroline were next to each other. "I hope," said she, "you are improving, Mr. Fishback."

"Yes, I'm a bundance better, but I can't bear no weight on my left leg yet. Miss Calline, I thought o' you a heap since

I was here that time; seems to me like you git purtier and purtier."

"Oh, Mr. Fishback, you are *such* a flatterer—how many young ladies have you spoken to in the same manner since you were last here?"

"Narry one, dad fetched ef I have. I never makes game o' no umurn—allers says what I think, and think jest what I say, —nigger fetch me one o' them thar flitters;" (this remark had reference to some fritters Mrs. Graves had prepared for dessert, and were placed on a table in the corner of the room but which our unposted hero proposed to mix with the large supply of meat and greens to which he had been helped.)

"Of course, you gentlemen never fail in bringing to bear a sufficient amount of plausibility to demonstrate your own sincerity." This sentence smelt a little too strong of the dictionary for Fishback to quite understand its signification; so, rather than venture a reply that might be inappropriate, he merely observed, "that's what *you* say."

"Yes indeed, and it's so. Now, Mr. Fishback, I appeal to your candor,—isn't it?"

"You aint heard me say it was—fetch me a flitter, nigger, can't you hear nothin?—niggers is a mighty pester."

Thus they went on chatting and eating, until our hero made the scholarly announcement that he was "chock full," and the rest felt the force of the same interesting truth.

Fishback now became a lame convalescent, limping about the house and occasionally a short distance up the road. His appearance among the young ladies was a signal for all to retire excepting "Calline." With her, and in fact with the whole family, he had now no equal.

Brother Jack was informed by letter, that "sister Caroline was going to marry a gentleman of immense wealth and a member of the Georgia Legislature." His fame was noised through the settlement, and ladies were constantly dropping in "just to make a pop-call, see if the family were well and hear the news;" but with no other real object than that of catching a glimpse of the newly discovered prodigy. Each carried home her opinion, and dealt it out like a faithful commissary. Mrs. Brown "considered him a barbarian monster; he couldn't begin to roost round her; she'd bet he'd give all the Graveses the itch." Kate Henry "knew *he* was no member of the Legislature; she'd bet he couldn't find the way there." Jennie Lee "was really surprised at Caroline Graves for reading that letter to everybody until it was nearly worn out by finger-marks—had a great mind to tell her it was an arrant forgery, and he nothing more nor less than a deserter. Why he smelt *so offensive*, with the tobacco juice running out at both corners of his mouth, he was absolutely hideous; she had no doubt he was at home a penniless and unprincipled vagabond." Miss Sallie Davis "thought he ought to be named Count D'Orsay Chesterfield, he was such a model man in dress and manners; oh, he did converse so charmingly about his 'mammy' and his 'crap,' his 'taters, warter-millions' etc.; *he* was a honey." Thus did envious neighbors berate the lordly lover of the fortunate Caroline. But she lived in blissful ignorance of their denunciations. Indeed, since scarcely a lady called without threatening to steal him from her or passing some other such compliment, she entertained no doubt that he was an object of general admiration. Gilbert Van, a young man of limited means, but fine attainments and decided promise, who had been paying court to her, now saw his orb pass into total eclipse behind the rising splendors of the illustrious Fishback. Minnows must clear the track when whales are afloat. Our hero's object now was to marry Caroline and induce the Major to sell his real property, crop and all, for the purpose of settling on his (Fishback's) unoccupied lands in Georgia. After the marriage and sale should be accomplished, he would take his wife, the negroes and most of the money, and leave for Georgia, letting the Major remain behind with his family a few weeks until he could get fixed up for him. At some convenient point on the route, he intended selling the negroes, leaving his wife (as he had no use for one,) and traveling to parts unknown. But he properly suspected that before trusting him so implicitly, the Major would want a little more evidence on the subject of his wealth and standing at home. For the purpose of supplying this deficiency, he frequently sat for hours by the road side waiting to find among the passing stragglers a suitable accomplice. While Fishback was planning for the future, however, and the neighbors comparing his claims to respectability, time was rolling on, and the shy, modest Caroline growing impatient to get courted. Our hero, who still remembered the admonition of Squalls, was too humane to allow her suspense to continue. So, one evening, as they sat in the piazza together, he drew his chair close to hers and remarked, "I swear pine blank, Calline, I luv you better'n any young umurn I ever seed."

"Ah, Mr. Fishback, you know you're just flattering me."

"No, I'll be dad blasted ef I am. I luved you the first time I ever seed you, and ef you'l jest marry me, no troubles shan't never bother you no more. Say yes, that's a purty gal?"

With a woman's disposition to evade giving the answer, she dreads, and yet longs to make, Miss Caroline replied in an affectionate and entreating manner: "Why don't you let them elect you to the Legis .... there, now."

"Run me for what? been into that pocket-book o' mine, ah?"

"Now, Mr. Fishback," speaking excitedly, "let me tell you exactly how it happened—"

"No you needn't, hunny, its all right, but I was *mightly* in hopes no body wouldn't see them papers; say, what you're gwine to do about havin me?"

"*You're not in earnest*; you want some of those charming Georgia girls."

"Drat the infernal Georgy gals, they ain't fit to tote guts to a bar! Say, answer the question; won't you marry me?"

Miss Caroline laughed, grew red, and finally subsiding into seriousness, replied: "It is an important matter, and you must allow me a day or two to reflect and make up my mind."

"Well, hunny," said he, looking at her affectionately, and speaking as gently as he could, "all right, but don't keep me in expense longer as you can help it, for I shall be mighty worried twel you let me know."

The young ladies were now summoned to the parlor, (and in going for them Caroline told all that passed, with incredible rapidity,) and the evening was shortened by mirth and music. Time thus killed, dies a chloroform death. It glides away bearing a blissful, sweet unconsciousness that it is passing. But I have no *time* for digression.

About sunset a soldier came to the yard gate and hailed.

Fishback usually acted the porter familiar, on such occasions, but now appearing to feel so intensely happy in his present position, he waited for Major Graves to answer the summons. "Can I stay here to-night?" spoke the man as the Major opened the door.—

"Stop," said Fishback, to the ladies. "I've hearn that voice, —stop your blasted pyanner, and lemme listen."

"Not well," replied the Major, "we are poorly prepared for company, at this time, two miles ahead you will find a good house to stop at."

"Well, but my dear sir, I am so egregiously fatigued—", our hero listened no further; rushing through the door, he ran out, and the two friends met and shook hands in the most "transporting, rapturous" manner;—"How de Isick, how de do old feller, come in a hepe." Having introduced Mr. Slaughter,—for such was the name borne by that individual—to the family, he made him lift off his harness and seat himself among the family.

"Well, Billy," said he, "it has been some time since we met before, and both of us have doubtless passed through a fearful ordeal during the eventful and sanguinary interim."

"You heerd my horn blow, big sis," was the appropriate and forcible reply of the quick-witted Fishback.

"But the lowering future is yet ominous of events in which we, perchance, will be integrals of a most belligerent aggregation."

"That's jest *my* notions."

"And perhaps we may become the doomed victims of a cruel, relentless and crucifying bellicosity."

"That's the very thing I was gwine to a sed."

"But, though we should fall, it is consoling to reflect that the liberty for which we have struggled, is progressive, diffusive and eternal."

"Them's the same words I've been thinkin about, right-smart while—when did you hear from Georgy?"

"I left home two weeks ago, today."

"Oh, yes," speaking sorrowfully, "I hearn o' that."

"Well, I believe there's nothing else in the way of news; yes, I received a telegraphic dispatch during my sojourn in Richmond, last Monday, stating that you had been unanimously elected to a seat in the Georgia House of Representatives, from our county."

"Won't have it, can't stand it, ain't a gwine to be pestered with no such."

"Yes, you must," whispered a female voice, accompanying its words with a look of melting tenderness.

"No, but I'll be dinged if I do; my country in the bog and me a sittin primpt up, like I was a havin my dod-drotted picter tuck; gal, you don't know what you'r talkin about—how's my crap a gittin on."

"Very well, indeed, very well; a more productive harvest has never been garnered on the premises than that which is at present ripening. Your estate has been appraised at near one hundred and fifty thousand dollars, (according to the gold and silver basis) and it is reported that the outstanding liabilities amount to less than fifteen hundred dollars; really, my dear Fishback, you have enough to commence life comfortably, with your economy and good financiering qualities, a large fortune will certainly be accumulated."

Yes, I've got enough to scrouge along with ef I can only git a good, savin wife." At this he ogled Caroline, who let her eyes drop, and looked, for all the world, like she meant to try and make a "savin wife."

"You might add considerably to your capital stock by effecting a union with the rich and literary heiress, Miss Julia Evans. It is reported that she's in the incipient stages of dementation, on your account."

"She be darnd; Jule Ivins' been tryin to git me a mighty long time."

"But she can't do it, can she?" tenderly whispered a soft voice.

"No, indeed, mam," said Slaughter, replying to the question; "although she is wealthy, intelligent and justly accounted a star of the first magnitude among the queenly luminaries of that refulgent clime, yet I venture to say that our friend Fishback is peculiarly the proprietor of his own heart, which will never be bartered for gold or splendor."

"I commend Mr. Fishback for that," said she, "for of all unpardonable violations of the laws of our being, I regard mercenary love the most unpardonable. It is like selling, not our brother Joseph, but our very selves into perpetual bondage."

"You are correct. It is indeed, an imitation of Judas—bartering immortality for a sum of money. We are not the owners of the soul, and have no right to vend it—that eternal element has been entrusted to us as custodians only; a truth which we find beautifully illustrated in the parable of the talents—if we bury it in the cumbrous rubbish of filthy lucre, how fearful will be the ulterior consequences?"

"If I can but have true affection in an humble home, I'll never be willing to exchange it for all the pompous wretchedness wealth can purchase."

"I endorse the sentiment most cordially. Bribe the needle to play truant to the pole—train the untrameled wind to blow not 'where it listeth'—teach the thirsty sun-beam to leave undrunk the dews of heaven, but this heart must revolve in its allotted periphery, or cease to move."

Although, so far as we know, our hero was wholly unacquainted with any foreign language, he had caught the gist of this conversation, and now ventured his own sentiments on the subject, in the following laconic style: "I'll be dad blasted ef I hadn't ruther try to set on a dozen rotten eggs twel I hatcht the last one uv 'em, as to marry a umurn jest for her munny, and spect to git along; thar aint narry bit o' use a tryin. Hit's like cetchin a jack-a-ma-lantern; it looks powerful easy, but hit haint no go. I shant marry for nuthin but love"—looking significantly at Caroline,—"dad blasted ef I do."

The conversation continued for some time, Slaughter occasionally "piling the agony" on Fishback who manifested the most dignified indifference to worldly honors. It is said that our hero was several times embarrassed by forgetting the name of his *intimate friend*, which he explained away in a satisfactory manner by saying his "Mammy had whipt him so much when he was little, about callin folks by thar names he'd got so he couldn't recollect nobody's name." This rumor, however, is so variant from the character of our hero that we pronounce it a flagrant slander. The two friends occupied the same bed that night, and both rose early next morning.

"You must pay me *Fifty* dollars for my services, Fishback," remarked Slaughter.

"Why, you said you'd tend to it for ten dollars and lodgin."

"I know I did, but I've reconsidered; certainly a man should have the privilege of changing his mind. I have managed your case so successfully that I am satisfied fifty dollars will be but a paltry remuneration."

"Can't pay you but ten."

"Very well, I'll settle my own bill, unsay all I have said, and we'll separate as we met. That, of course, will be satisfactory, since the terms of settlement can't be agreed upon."

"I'll give you twenty-five: aint got narry nuther cent ef I had to be hung."

"That's all satisfactory, perfectly so; we'll just rue the trade and leave the matter where it stood before I came; this can be accomplished pleasantly enough by just telling what passed between us up the road yesterday. As for taking less than *fifty*, I couldn't entertain such an idea. My price or the original status, are the only alternatives I can accept, and either will be entirely agreeable to me."

"Ef I borry the fifty for you will you put in some more o' them jodarters about me bein a good egg?"

"Yes, I'll branch out on the subject of your disposition, at the breakfast table, and make a few additional remarks on points already canvassed, if the fifty is in hand; but as you haven't got the money convenient, I have no objections to canceling the contract; don't, I conjure you, don't raise the money just for my accommodation. I'd prefer to rescind."

It is needless to say, the spondulics were forthcoming. Breakfast and the purchased praises having been faithfully completed, Slaughter's haversack was filled, and he passed on.

Fishback's character was now established by concurring testimony, in which there could have been no collusion, and Caroline found herself urged by the family and her *ardent affection*, to consummate the proposed marriage, with the least possible delay. The Major readily consented to offer his real property for sale,—move from the borders to the Georgia interior, and settle on the rich wiregrass lands of his future son-in-law. Our hero, likewise, after much persuasion, finally yielded a reluctant consent to pull loose from the warm embraces of "grim-visaged war," and "caper nimbly" in the Legislature. Whereupon, Thursday, the twelfth day of Octo-

ber, was fixed upon as the happy, nuptial day. The Major
was so anxiously urged by every member of his family, present and prospective, to sell out on any terms, that in less
than one week after his lands were put upon the market, he
had passed a title, and received as the whole purchase money,
a sum so inadequate as, only for the bright prospect ahead,
would have made him feel ruined. But Fishback knew where
better lands could be procured for half the amount; he
(Fishback) had consented to take the money and thus in-
vest it, and the Major felt so happy that the trade had
been completed, that he almost made a boy of himself.

Time moved on, and the wedding day, for which our
hero longed most monstrously, drew near. Invitations went in
every direction, and the Graveses and their neighbors, were
all astir. The ladies in the settlement, including Mrs. Brown
and Misses Lee, Henry and Davis gave active aid in preparing for the great event. One of Caroline's dresses—a jaconet
muslin—underwent slight repairs, and was set apart for the
wedding night, and a fine, flowered silk, for the day succeeding. Fishback had obtained, the day before his arrival, all
the necessary equipments to make a very respectable marriage
suit; the pants, it is true, not having been cut for him, were
rather short and a little too tight around the ankle, or rather,
above it, for they didn't reach quite that far down. But that
was a matter of no consequence. Cakes and sweet things
of every variety and in great profusion were undergoing
the process of preparation. The Major stated that "this was
to be, not only a wedding, but a farewell supper, in which he
intended his friends should feast to fullness." The truth is
he had never been so elated at any event of his life, as the
prospect of a wealthy son-in-law and a body of rich Georgia
lands, and therefore, felt like it was his time to stand treat.

The evening before the wedding day, one of the young
ladies ran into our hero's room and resting her hand on his
shoulder, began: "Oh, I'm so happy, I've just got a letter
from brother Jack, and he'll be here to-morrow; now, won't
you help us persuade him to move to Georgia,—won't you,
my good brother, William?"

"Yes, we'll take him along—how much land's he got?"

"About four hundred acres, papa says."

"Let him sell out at half price, and I'll take his money and buy twist as much land in Georgy, and hit clerd and fenst, and better'n his'n."

"Now, if you'l only manage to make brother understand that, and get him to go with us, I promise to be *the best sister*."

"All right, I'll fix that pint."

It seemed now that riches were actually crowding themselves upon the fortunate Fishback. In three days he was to start for the South with the Major's money, daughter and negroes, leaving the Major himself to sell a small remnant of his crop, which was yet undisposed of, (while the remainder of the family paid a few parting visits,) and bring them on afterwards. Now, he determined that the credulous Jack should let *his* lands, negroes and produce drift into the same channel. Charmed with the pleasing prospect, he felt that he could hardly wait for the slow motioned Time, and again did he rehearse in two minutes, the weighty arguments he would wield on that occasion; the earnestness and force with which he would urge immediate action, in view of another invasion, and the persuasive influence that might be expected from the family. The theme was thrillingly delightful, and he dwelt on it with the rapture of an enthusiast.

The morning of the twelfth at length came on, and was clear, pleasant, and marked by no jostling variation from the steady progress with which events were ripening, except that, perhaps, Miss Caroline felt a greater flutter in the region of her heart, than she had before experienced, and the Major's stove-pipe hat was somewhat slicker than usual. The hour of one o'clock came, dinner was ready, and was about to be commenced—several visiting ladies present, among whom were Misses Lee and Henry, were "up to their eyes" in business, and our hero with his affianced sat in the parlor, their hands locked together, and their eyes and voices expressing infinite happiness; when suddenly the cry arose, "brother Jack's come! brother Jack's come!" and the female Graveses charged "the big gate," and swarmed around him. Each began at the same time, and in the most impatient manner to herald the praises of their inchoate husband and brother. "I know you'll love him, brother Jack," said Caroline, "he's so good and so noble." "Yes, and he's fine looking," remarked another; "and pa thinks," observed a third, "that he's a gentleman of great solidity of character, the first order of business talents and remarkably good judgment." Thus they moved on slowly, each trying to out talk the rest.

Fishback sat at the window, straining his eyes to catch a glimpse of the notorious Jack, who was yet hid by the intervening grove; he felt great anxiety to see whether that gentleman possessed a persuadable physiognomy. Presently his anxious eyes were rewarded by the coveted sight. Having passed from behind some paradise trees in about ten steps of the house, he came in full view, and oh! terrific truth, that brother was none other than the black-whiskered, pock-marked man who had behaved in such blood-thirsty manner at Mrs. Lane's. There was no time to be lost. He sprang out at the window with a violence that disturbed his equilibrium. "La," said one of the young ladies, "what a frightful fall Mr. Fishback's got!" "I'm afraid it hurt him," observed the sympathetic Caroline, starting herself to his relief. But the hero of our story was a goner. Having rushed through the back yard, he soon became lost to view in the neighboring woods, leaving his hat, pocket-book and washing to be attended to by the Graveses; his adorable "Calline" to be commended for her discernment and sagacity, by the firm of Mrs. Brown & Co., and the wedding guests to play a long, pleasant and interesting game of Criticism.

CHAPTER VI

In which our Hero wabbles himself into a scrape under the tormenting influence of sore temptation and is extricated by virtue of his own address and management, and after a series of adventures, finally merges into a terrible fight, which terminates in ...., another Chapter.

Reader, imagine yourself the sentient soul of a family circle, blessed with the "first and passionate love" of a young, beautiful and accomplished woman, about to be lifted from the slough of extreme poverty, into the feathered lap of opulence. View yourself caressed and fondled by the leaders of fashion, lionized by all grades and classes of society, serenaded by the musical rustles of silk, and breathing the aromas of cologne and musk; in short, an acknowledged gentleman of the first water, so tenderly preserved that the croaking of frogs is not permitted to grate upon the delicate tympanum, nor the winds of Heaven to take any disgusting liberties with your person. Then behold yourself shoved from this giddy pinnacle, with a smashing fall, and set adrift upon the world without purse or scrip; hatless, houseless, rationless, and, in short, altogether empty, seedy, and forsaken—an Adam ejected from his earthly Paradise. Yea, verily, a Cain, seeking refuge from the abodes of men; and as you reflect that such was now the situation of William Fishback, let your tears—those dove-like messengers sent forth from the Ark of the heart, to bear witness to a sunken, ruined world, that emotions, tender and gushing, yet survive the wreck of nature, and the floods and storms of passion and ambition; your tears, the rain that descends from the heaven of the eye, to fructify the soul, let your tears come down in sloshes.

Our friend, Rufe Bates, has told us, "that marriage is often the result of venial and unnoticeable accident." Now, close the book, shut your eyes, and by reflecting a little, you will observe, that in this instance, the contrary effect has resulted from the same kind, quality and nicely woven texture of accidents as those to which he referred. The stately and dignified Bones, although he champs his clover in profound unconsciousness of his own importance, you will find to have been the mainspring in this dissolving machine. But, we have no time to follow the train of suggestions thus presented. We must pursue the spoor of our wandering and friendless hero. *We*, at least, will not forsake him.

The extent of Fishback's panic, is almost incredible to relate. For some time, he crept through the country, traveling mostly at night, and never venturing to let day-light catch him on a public road. What were his meditations during this eventful period, we have not been permitted to know. Chained down in the dark dungeon of his mind, they are doomed, perhaps, to a perpetual imprisonment. To burst the bars of this impregnable prison, is not a work for arms as weak as ours; nor to illumine its benighted cells, a task that can be accomplished by the dim and flickering lights which we possess. These meditations will, therefore, have to remain for the nonce invisible inhabitants of an imperceptible home.

His object was now, to terminate the wanderings and uncertainties of his life, by once more connecting himself with the company to which he belonged, then stationed (as was the balance of the army) near Winchester, for which purpose,—compelled by the advance of the Federals,—he took a circuitous route, passing through Culpepper, Madison and the Luray Valley.

As time and distance molified the enormity of his terrors, he began, by degrees, to show himself on the high road and in open daylight. Cavalry details, in search of stragglers, had, of late, infested the neighborhood, and occasionally visited the residence of Major Graves, a circumstance that learned our hero to carry about his person the discharge he had procured; which was, therefore, not left behind in his hasty exodus. With it, he felt protected against the probability of arrest, but he could not catch himself falling in with a whiskered man, that he did not shudder. During this time, our hero, with his usual purveying strategy, had kept every want supplied; but now, that he had reached the track over which the army trains, together with the loafers, stragglers, "green apple rifles," "persimmon rogues" and "hospital grad-

uates," were constantly traveling, the country was so thoroughly eaten out, it became next to impossible for him to draw
supplies. Under the circumstances, he resolved to avail himself of the first horse he could lay hands on, to hurry forward.

One morning, just after he descended the mountain, on
the Page county side, he passed a fine looking residence, near
which he saw several stout horses standing in a lot. This was
a sight that made him pause. How to make himself master of
one, was, of course, an engrossing subject of reflection. At
this moment a soldier came out of the gate with a canteen of
apple brandy. "Whar did you sneak on that ar, mister?"
asked our hero.

"I got it out of that old man's cellar, but *you* can't git
a drop. I had to lie and beg both, besides paying a smart
price."

"I shant tell no lies, but ef he's got any more, hit's mine.
I'm a gwine a purpose—reckon I'll catch you." So saying, he
passed on, and in a few moments more was in the presence
of Capt. Royal, the proprietor of the place, a tall, dignified
benevolent looking gentleman of sixty. "How much do you
ask for your sperits, mister?" said Fishback.

"I haven't a drop for sale, sir," replied the Captain, "I
just now let a soldier have a quart, under circumstances of
great emergency, but I can't possibly let any more go. I
have not enough left to supply the medicinal necessities of
my family, now that we are cut off from our usual supply
of medicines."

"Mighty sorry for it, got seven men out here a mile
and better, all wounded at Shephardstown. The Doctor sent
me to carry 'em to Culpepper, and gin me money and told
me to buy sperits for 'em. Three ov em's broke down, and
most obliged to die—thought maybe you'd sell me a little,
and I'd git 'em well enough so I could tote 'em to that yonder
old out house, (ef you'd let 'em lie in it) twell they mended
up a little, then I'd hunt round and hire a wagin to take em
on to Culpepper. Maybe by givin em spirits and totin em, I
might git em this fur. Hit's mighty bad to be wounded and lay
out in the cold and die. Spozen you step down and see em?"

"Certainly, certainly, I'll go and bring them to my house,
and nurse them like a father until they are able to travel.

Bob"—calling to his servant,—"hitch the horses to the wagon, put in a mattress, and drive around to the front gate."

The wagon soon made its appearance at the place designated, and our hero having instructed Bob to "turn them hosses' heads tother way," assured the Captain that he didn't "feel like gwine back to them fellers without something to liven em up on; one ov em, he knowed, was so sick twell he couldn't ride in a wagin thout sumthin to drink twell he got better."

"Sure enough," replied the sympathetic and tender-hearted Captain, "I like to have forgotten the brandy; they *must* have some of that, and everything else I possess calculated to relieve or comfort them, bring on your canteen, stranger." Having led the way into his cellar, he filled the canteen and handed it to our hero, who stepping out quickly, locked the door and put the key in his pocket, leaving the Captain safe on the inside. How long he remained in durance vile or whether he devoted the period of his incarceration to commisserating the situation of the seven wounded soldiers, we positively do not know. Fishback had no sooner reached the wagon, than he began to berate Bob most violently for not hurrying to his master, who was certainly at that moment calling loudly. Bob started to apologize by saying that he didn't hear "massa," and that "de hosses wouldn't stand 'dout sumbody to hold em—"

"Be off you black devil, and don't stand here a jawin me; I'll hold your hosses, glong, run, or I'll bust your brains out." This gentle observation was accompanied with such a menacing gesture and fierce grimaces, that Cuffie, not waiting for the slow process of passing through the gate, vaulted the fence and went gracefully trotting to his master. During this time, our hero had been hastily unbuckling the harness from the saddle horse, and now quickly slipped it off and rode away in triumph.

Up to this period, Fishback had not slept in a bed since his departure from the Graves mansion. There prevailed such an amount of measles, camp-itch, small-pox and villainy among the straggling gang, that a footman could no more crowd himself into one of these comfortable sleeping places than a Camel could pass through the eye of an Irish potato, so to speak. Now, however, since he had risen in the world, our hero resolved to pass, if possible, the succeeding night where he could enjoy the luxuries of a roof and a bed. With this object in view, he rode up about deep dusk, to the residence of Mr. Stapleton, an old bachelor, living eight miles beyond Luray, and one mile off the Strasburg road, and, having hitched his horse, walked in. As he started up the piazza steps, he saw a gentleman dressed in a Captain's uniform, sitting just inside the nearest room-door, and being—like other stragglers,—afraid of officers, he turned to leave, intending to get away before he was seen; when he heard the Captain remark to Stapleton: "Inferences are excluded from the analytical dissection of metaphysical topics. Madam Necker truly observes, 'les limites des sciences sont comme l'horizon, plus en approche, plus elles reculent.' They are boundless as space, fathomless as infinity, and limitless as the range of conception."

Fishback paused, "them words is Slaughter's," thought he, "nobody never said no sich, but him."

"The clime of Utopia is alone congenial to the growth, expansion and development of doubts, speculations and uncertainties. They yield to the power of dialects, like a gossamer to the sturdy stroke of a giant—"

"Sich a dod-dratted fool. Wonder what creek he catcht them big words outen?"

"There is no such reality as an occult science. Because a man loses his eye-sight, is no reason why he should proclaim that the luminous world is an occult and benighted globe. The fault exists in the vision, not in the great, eternal and immutable principle."

"Whar on yeath is the fool-killer? he ought to be cashsheared for bein outen place. Oh yes, hits Slaughter. Allers talkin grammer, and I can cheat him outen his eye-teeth. Sich talk as that don't do no good. Wonder whar he stold them Cap'n's fixins?"

"Anaxagoras and Zoroaster, in their earnest search after divine truth, doubtless thought it enveloped in a maze of mystery; the light of revelation shone as brightly then as it shines today, but they were permitted to see only as through a glass darkly; *their visions* (not the light) were obstructed, after they culminated with beatified spirits, in the empyrean splendors of the celestial Canaan, restrained no longer by the feeble retina of a clay-beclouded spiritual vision, they beheld a universe crowded with eternal and un-changeable certainties, which have shone with indiminished resplendency through the world's long ages of darkness and storm."

This was "talk enough" for our hero. Walking into the piazza, he boldly inquired, "Is Captain Slaughter here?" The Captain *pro-tem*, who had no idea of being officially addressed in a strange voice, involuntarily sprang to his feet, under the influence of considerable agitation. Fishback observed this, and apprehensive lest it might result in his being ignored, rushed forward, and grabbing Slaughter by the right hand in both of his, seemed ready to swoon under the ecstasy of his love. "Why how do you do, Cap'n, how de do, how de do, I'm *so* glad to see you! Was *so* feared you was a sufferin. The Colonel told me to hunt you up, and find out how you was a gittin, and tell you about your being promoted to Lieut. Colonel; he said you was the best officer in the army, and he didn't know how hard it was to get along without you till you left; said ef you wanted a furlough or money, jest send me after it, and it was yourn."

"Come, come, Billy," remarked Slaughter, after the usual salutations and introductions were completed. "Come, repair with me to my apartment, and divest yourself of those ac-coutrements, for I know you must be egregiously fatigued."

"Yes, I'm mighty much so: that blasted hard trottin hoss is enough to churn the chittlins outen a feller."

"Oh, did you ride? well, I'll see that your horse is at-tended to, after I dispose of you. How did you come out with Signor Graves' daughter? Did the fifty you paid me prove to be a profitable investment?"

"Oh, mighty, mighty—here Slaughter, take a nip at this canteen—hit's got some uv the peore tally-twisty: hit'l brighten a feller's caracter jest to rub up agin it."

So far was our hero from being a professional drinker, that the canteen yet remained almost as full as when he brought it from the cellar; but the pseudo Captain, who, among his many virtues, had never boasted power enough to resist the influence of this temptation,—warmed his inner man with a big drink. "Now," said he, starting out of the room, "make yourself comfortable here, until I look after your jaded and way-worn steed."

In about half an hour Slaughter returned, the two friends again imbibed and repaired to supper. After completing the table duties, as the night was pleasant, and the moon shone brightly, they strolled together for the purpose of swapping secrets, and Slaughter opened the conversation in this wise: "Fishback, notwithstanding my acquaintance with you is but limited, I propose to make an unreserved announcement of my future plans, provided you pledge me your sacred honor as a gentleman, that you will never reveal what I disclose, nor do any act calculated to thwart or impede the plan of operations I have concocted."

"Ding it all, Slaughter, I aint red them books that cum outen—don't talk none o' your grammar to me, I don't know half your a sayin."

"Well, then, if I tell you what I'm going to do, you give me your word of honor as a gentleman, never to tell one word I say to you, nor to do anything that will keep me from doing what I tell you I am going to do."

"You must think I'm a mean man, to think I'de do the like o' that. Yes, I'll promise never to say nothin about it, never bother nothin about it, ef it aint got no steelin uv my hoss in it. Think I'm a rascal do you?"

"No, Fishback, I am not questioning your integrity, but the observance of due precautions is a necessary preliminary to all successful undertakings."

"Now listen at you; you've got a mighty quality tongue, real ristercratic mouth, but I aint a hearin you."

"I said it was best not to make a blowing horn of what we're going to do; we should be careful, and particular about telling our secrets even to the purest men; it is best they should be under obligations of secrecy and fidelity."

"Oh yes, bleeve I know what that means. You're right; tell on, and ef I don't stand up to what I prommust, you may take my head and make a wast nest outen it. I've done some ugly tricks, but I allers was a honest man, and dad-blast me ef I don't mean to stay so—come, old fel, shoot your shickle."

"Well, what I have to say, will occupy but a minute. I

have managed to scrape together seven hundred dollars in gold, and next Monday, I will avail myself of a neighbor's absence, to get four hundred more, and during the night following, I design making my escape to Washington City, on Stapleton's fine horse, which I will show you as we walk back; he paces easier, runs faster, and looks prettier than any animal in the Luray Valley,—suppose we go back to the lot now and see him. I want to show him to you; but mind, you must speak in a low voice when you talk of these matters there; there's no calculating the ulterior consequences that would result from detection."

"Mind, look out, you'r about to fling up some more o' them big words."

In a few minutes, the two stood before the stable-door, looking upon a horse of such beauty and symmetry, such rounded, well-proportioned limbs and gracefully curving crest, as gave our hero a most insatiable appetite to be his owner.

"How you gwine to git him outen the stable? gwine to break down the door?"

"Oh, no! Stapleton would catch me at that. I know precisely where the key hangs, just inside of the back part of the corn-crib, which protrudes into the back yard—come, let me show you." They arrived directly at the place mentioned, when Slaughter, pointing to a crack just large enough for a man's arm to pass through, without leaving any margin of either width or breadth, remarked: "By reaching my arm into this crack, up to my shoulder, and feeling down to the floor and about ten inches from the logs, I can get the key any time. It always hangs, or rather, lies there. As Stapleton is frequently from home, and there is great uncertainty in letting it be thrown about the house, he has selected that as a point from which he and his servants will never fail to get it."

This conversation, carried on in a low cautious tone of voice, was now suddenly interrupted by the appearance of a negro mounted on Fishback's horse, and making his escape from the lot. Stapleton and his whole force ran out to aid in stopping the thief, but the lessening sound of his rattling hoofs soon admonished them to give over their endeavors. Our hero insisted on bouncing Stapleton's blooded horse to go in pursuit of him, but being informed that the by-paths and mountain-defiles were too numerous and intricate to afford any possibility of success, he gave over the undertaking, and accompanied his friend to the room they were to occupy, and the two continued to speak and prey upon Slaughter's plan of operations.

"Here," observed our hero, "take another drink, Slaughter, take a buster, ef you git drunk no body won't know it, but me."

"Billy, it doesn't take much liquor to affect me. I am now under the influence of what I drank before supper; but, nevertheless, here goes."

"Now, I'll give it a buss, and then we'll proceed—ain't you afraid somebody'l steal your money?"

"No, indeed, it's safe from intrusion, secure from molestation, absolutely and unconditionally safe and secure."

"I tell you, money's mighty slippery, hit's got wings bigger'n a buzzard, now a days, and flies away without flappin em, silent as a cat. Massy, that spirits is *so* good, gwine to take another drink right now and you've got to jine me, no gittin round it."

"I am already reeling, actually reeling, the foundations of the great deep of my equilibrium are broken up, but, for your sake I'll imbibe once more. Look here, my dear fellow, you must stay with me tomorrow, and I'll try and put you on track of another horse, but I conjure you not to misbehave while you remain here; you are welcomed as my friend, and I am therefore, responsible for your conduct. I entreat you to remember, that any violation of the strictest propriety, will have a tendency to thwart my plans, and will, therefore, constitute a violation of your sacred pledge."

"Slaughter, I tell you flat down, that I don't like for you to be a hintin that I'm a mean man; such as that don't set well on my stomach. Drink your spirits and let my character alone. Yes, I'm a gwine to stay with you to-morrow, and ef you keep bein as clever a feller as what I've found you, we'll allers be good friends. I'll stand up to you, Slaughter; dad dinged ef I wouldn't ruther die as to brake my promise; but this way you've got a hintin, hit's *got to be stopt*."

"Well, well, no harm, no harm; let's cure our differences with a draught; brandy is a sure antidote for poison."

On this occasion the canteen remained semi-vertical with

the little end in Slaughter's mouth, until he swallowed three times. Certain that drunkenness would speedily result from these multiplied and copious drinks, our hero began to feel, as do the heirs of a rich old bachelor uncle, when the doleful doctor solemnly announces that he's about to embark in the bucket-kicking business. "Are you right sure your money's safe? Whar did you put it? Don't want nothin to git lost while I'm stayin here."

"I always sleep with it under my head," replied Slaughter, thickening his speech to the consistency of curd, and feeling really a part of what he labored so industriously to put on. "I always sleep with it under my head—pecunia sub caput." Then falling on the bed and closing his eyes, he continued, "Behave yourself, most noble Fishy, and be not the dupe of treacherous cogitations. Remember with what odium the slave of Emperamus and the treacherous Epialtes suffered their names to drift down the current of history; remember these impious traitors and avoid their examples."

"Oh, yes; I remember hit. I'll do what's right. Your money aint under your pillar; better git up and git it; you'll be asleep in a minit." But Slaughter was now busily snoring, and our hero felt that he had over-reached himself in making the liquor take effect so soon, and was not a little provoked, that his chum should have gone to sleep without giving him some reliable information as to the geographical status of his gold. But his will was not one that yielded to trifles. Every place in the room, where money was likely to be put on general or special deposit, passed under the scrutiny of his eye. When this plan failed to accomplish the desired object, he pulled Slaughter out of bed and began, "Why the devil don't you pull off your clothes, and git under the kiver?"

"Do you suspect I'll refrigerate," asked Slaughter, in a muddy and almost unintelligible voice, as he began clumsily to aid in getting off his clothes. Fishback had hoped by undressing him to restore a partial wakefulness, until he could get some clue to the desired treasure; but his comrade did not once open his eyes during the whole time, and as soon as he was undressed, rolled under the cover, apparently, in a state of perfect unconciousness.

"Come, come," said our hero, "wake up; I aint done with

you yet. Git up and go this minute and git your money, and put it under your head. Don't you know the country's full o' rogues? Don't want nothin stold, while I'm here, to be laid on me. Go, get your money."

"Money *fuit non est nunc*," replied Slaughter, half opening his eyes, and gazing around in a foolish, sleepy, manner.

"Slaughter, go get your money; I swear some rogue'll get it afore day, and you'll be a layin it on me."

"Why, hallo Fishback, is that you? Where did you emerge from?"

"Slaughter don't ax no such foolish questions; get up," (shaking him) "and go get your money. Don't you know ef hit gets lost you're ruined. I know where it is. You know you told me all about it; but I'll be dad blasted ef I'm a gwine to be a handlin any body else's money, to have 'em accusin me uv stealin, ef any uv hit's gone."

"Fish," replied Slaughter, brightening up a little; "I've all pure confidence in your honesty; so, since you know where my money is, go get it and take care of it. Go, Fishy." Whereupon he closed his eyes, and persistently refused, thereafter, to allow either persuasion, scolds or pushing, to interrupt the melody of his snores.

It was now near midnight, and our hero, despairing of his object undressed and crept under the cover, when lo! he found himself lying on what, examination discovered to be, the veritable and much coveted bag of gold. In a minute more, he was on his feet, flung himself on the inside of Slaughter's military suit, took his (Slaughter's) new boots in one hand and the bag of gold in the other, and crept down stairs lightly as a cat. Having satisfied himself that everybody was asleep, he went cautiously to the back of the crib. With some difficulty he managed to work his arm into the crack above referred to, and having reached down until he brought himself to a laborious and uneasy tip-toe, he got the key between his thumb and finger and started to pull it out, when "snap" went a large steel-trap, which had been baited with the key and fastened to the floor; and our immortal hero was safe as a fish is, after he has swallowed the bait. Compelled to stand on tip-toe; tortured by the sharp teeth of the trap without any hope of deliverance or any human being on

whom he could call for succor, since it was evident that his
present predicament was the result of an inimical collusion
between Stapleton and Slaughter; the situation of our hero
was wretched in the extreme. But to add to the weight of his
woe, at this critical moment two huge dogs, which had
hitherto been kept down, came rushing forward and began
to tear his pants and mouth his person, with no very remarkable
delicacy of sentiment. Oh! he did need relief *so bad!* Slaughter
having swigged copiously of the canteen which Fishback
had left, and at the same time watched anxiously the movements of that gentleman, now reached his head from the
window and sang out, "beware, my dear sir, of those quadru-
peds; they are destructively voracious. I asseverate on my
honor that you are disagreeably circumstanced, but *cela ne me
fait vien du tout.*" This encouraging remark fell not on the
ears of Fishback, who was using his voice and remaining
hand in a wholly useless effort to better his condition. Every
time he kicked the dogs, the trap bit worse, and every time
he didn't kick them, they, of course, bit more severely.

Stapleton and Slaughter now approached the seat of
war. Their appearance gave additional fierceness to the dogs,
and a scene opened which language is much too tame and
spiritless to describe.

"Bow-wow-wow, yo-yo-yo-yo," said the dogs, as they
swung partners with the straitened Fishback. "Why don't
you take—leg-go—be off—your dogs away," replied the hero
of our story. "Yo-yo-yo-yo," resumed the loquacious canines.
"You—be ashamed—quit. I'll shoot your blasted"—"yo-yo-yo-
yo"—"dogs livers outen 'em."

"Why, really, friend Fish," observed Slaughter, "they seem
to be taking some rather disgusting liberties with your cap-
taincy; but it's their nature, my dear sir,—their primeval disposition—carniverous mammals possess abnormal ferocity."

"Why, Mr. Fishback," said Stapleton, speaking in a tone
sickeningly polite, "my dogs are behaving quite ungenteely,
quite so."

"Yo-yo-yo"—"oh my leg! my leg—go off—you, I'll shoot
your"—"yo-yo-yo-yo" "you—be off—your dogs' brains out."
"Take 'em off and—you," "yo-yo-yo-yo," "let me tell you one
thing"—

"Be off you rascals," said Stapleton, using the same politeness to his dogs, he had observed towards our hero; and in a tone too mild and unauthoritative to even attract their attention.

"Yea, verily," said the now reeling Slaughter, "I would advise all dogs to forego the pleasure of trespassing upon the rights of persons; and that reminds me of an anecdote once told on Count Rumford—"

"Yo-yo-yo"—continued the mastiffs—"blast your nanicdotes; the dogs is a killin me; you—be off—I've lost more'n—be gone—five gallons uv blood—oh, my leg—"

"You see, Mr. Fishback," remarked Stapleton, speaking as before, "I can't stop the dogs. Why do you not climb up the house?"

"How kin I"—"wow-wow yo-yo-yo"—"when the steeltrap's a—oh, cuss the dogs—holdin me straight up and down."

"A steel-trap! oh, indeed, why, if you had only let me known you wanted to put your hand into that crack I would, by no means, have been so impolite as to have left a steeltrap in an attitude so threatening; were you walking in your sleep, my dear sir?"

"No I was—" "yo-yo-yo," continued the unremitting chorus of the dogs, "tryin—be off—to git some more corn for my hoss—be off, take off your—drat 'em—dogs—"

"Why, bless me, what a mistake; you accidentally put on the Captain's uniform and—what's this lying by you? You must have been visiting the end of a rainbow."

"*Hic jacet pecunia*," remarked the staggering Slaughter.

"I was jest a—oh pray—please take off your—you—leggo my leg—take off your dogs. I was jest a playin a prank on Slaughter, I'd a give 'em back. Why don't you take off your —you, please, oh pray"—"yo-yo-yo-yo-yo-yo." "Oh, murder, murder; I'm dead! they've bit out my bowels. I'm dead, dead, dead! Tell mammy I died—oh oh! uh!"

This was delivered in a style so plaintively theatrical, it had the desired effect. The trap and dogs were disengaged, and our poor, persecuted hero, to all human appearances helpless and unconcious, was carried to the house and laid on a pallet. Stapleton felt alarmed, lest he had carried the joke too far; but Slaughter, in no situation to be foolishly prudent, insisted that "deceit being the primary ingredient in the disease, it cannot terminate fatally. As a proof of the correctness of my diagnosis, I propose to stick a pin in his corpus, and thus test the reality of its inertness." Just at this moment, (strange coincidence) Fishback opened his eyes, stared vacantly, and began to talk at random. "Mr. Stapleton," continued Slaughter, "if you will re-allow me the use of your dogs and trap, I will renew strength and precipitate locomotion in the enfeebled Fishback, upon the well established principle that 'the hair of the dog is good for the bite.'" Our hero began to exhibit strong symptoms of returning reason, and even raised himself on his elbow. "Let me see your wounds, Mr. Fishback," remarked the uneasy Stapleton, "and put some linament on them."

"No, no, let me alone, nothin can't save me. You've murdered a poor, innersent man, a fiten fur his country. But it don't matter. It'll all soon be over. I'm in hopes no body won't find out nothin about who done it, when I'm dead. I don't die with no ill will agin nobody." Stapleton's eyes filled with tears, and he was preparing to deliver a long apology, when he was pushed aside by Slaughter, who made two stout negroes hold our hero *vi et armis*, until every rag of clothes was stripped off of him from his head to his feet. Fishback struggled manfully against this, and would have run, but for the strength and tightness with which he was clutched; for after all the barking, growling and gnawing, his entire body was found to contain but one single dog bite that drew blood; and it was on the calf of his leg, and not larger than a silver quarter. This, added to the print of teeth faintly visible in several places, and occasional grainings of the skin, composed the sum total of his bodily sufferings, excepting the scar produced on his left hand by the trap. After making him swear never to reveal what had passed—a measure dictated by the prudent apprehensions of Slaughter, his horse was ordered; but the negro who had been instructed to ride him off in the early part of the night was over-acting his part, and had gone his way to return no more. Under the circumstances, Fishback was offered lodgings until morning, when all prospects of regaining his horse being lost, he took a cold snack in his hand, walked about two miles, and coiled himself

down in a fence corner, where he slept until late in the after-
noon, and again resumed his lonely march—suffering no little
with his swollen hand and bruised leg.

About dark, he came upon a horse hitched by the road
side, and advanced to take possession of him, when the surly
demand of "who's that?" from a person lying five, or six feet
off, arrested his movements. "Hit's me," he replied, at the
same time advancing to the horse's head and fingering the
headstall, "a hungry, tired, wounded soldier, hurryin back to
my command. I seed your hoss was about slippin his bridle,
and I stept by to fix it."

"Who the devil's me?"

"What business is that uv your'n. I'm a man, and a white
man, lives at home and boards at the same place—takes no
idvantige and ax's no odds uv no body. Got any more questions to ax?"

The boldness of this remark, so chimed in with the
reckless, daring spirit of the stranger, that he opened his
haversack and his blankets, and soon after, his heart itself to
our trustworthy hero.

Fishback went through with a long rigmarole about
Slaughter, Stapleton—the stolen horse—Stapleton's blooded steed
and the bag of gold, mixing a few grains of truth with a
vast amount of fiction. After which, they arranged a somewhat ingenious plan to secure the bag of gold and the racer,
during next day. To-morrow's campaign being thus planned,
and many superfluous suggestions made, discussed and rejected,
to allay the stranger's uneasiness about the safety of his horse,
they began to sleep and guard by reliefs, at which tedious
process the night dragged wearily away.

It so happened that day dawn found our hero on post
anxiously scrutinizing the features of his companion, whom
he discovered to be no less a personage than Squalls, of Wheat's
Battalion. This was a most agitating discovery. He had never
seen a man before—Jack Graves excepted—whose presence
shook his frame with such an earth-quake of terrors, as this
same fierce, impetuous, merciless, diabolical Squalls. Cautiously
strapping on Squalls' haversack—for he was nervously afraid
that semi-demon would awake and recognize him—our hero
saddled and mounted the horse, and now, of course, feeling

himself above the atmosphere of danger, called out in a voice loud enough to awake the sleeper, "say, mister, hit's day. I'll ride to the branch and water your hoss." "All right," replied Squalls, pulling the blanket over his head, preparatory to another snooze; and thus leaving the lower part of his body—which was doubled up tightly as a man's fist—fully exposed to view.

For a moment, our hero hesitated; then riding a short distance up the road, he cut and trimmed a long switch. "Now's my time," he observed, "to git even for the way he sarved me. I'll be outen retch o' his ketchin, afore he gets done rubbin whar it smarts. This is a mighty spirited hoss—dang it how my hand hurts."

Reader, unless you hunger and thirst after vengeance upon your enemies, unless your soul revels in the most exhilarating ecstasies at the prospect of revenge, you can form no conception of Fishback's feelings, as he rode almost over his victim, and began to sway his switch in the air, preparatory to the intended stroke. At length, bending down as far as possible, he drew back his arm and brought the switch to bear with all the power he possessed, upon the tightly wadded and unprotected part of Squalls' body, inflicting a cut that outstung a regiment of hornets. The horse seeing the descending whip, just at the time our hero bent furthest, made a wild jump—the saddle turned and with his feet dangling in the stirrups, our hero fell to the ground. Furious eyes bore down on him—a gleaming dirk was within six inches of his throat—a knee of power planted on his breast, and forsaken by his accustomed self-possession, he closed his eyes, that he might not witness his own murder.

CHAPTER VII

In which our hero is made the sport of circumstances—Experiences the fickleness of fortune—Meets Captain Smith—They do not embrace at first sight—Fishback takes lodgings in his old Richmond boarding house—Changes rooms and is finally lost sight of, while almost in the very act of "winking out."

The conclusion of the last chapter left our reader trembling for the fate of Fishback. We do not regard such abrupt terminations as befitting the style of serious biographies like that in which we are engaged; and we are therefore half inclined to apologise for what we have done. We are great on apologies. We once apologized so effectually to a gentleman who accidentally stepped on our toes, that he at length began to regard himself aggrieved, and finally became enraged to such an extent, that we had to get a friend to hold him. We could have apologized him into a good humor, but he wouldn't listen to us. In this instance, however, we prefer to explain rather than apologize.

Well then, to proceed. As we wound up or rather broke off the closing sentence of the last chapter, an old friend stepped in to give us an hour's chat, and an invite to his wedding. Now, we make it a point to finish a chapter at every sitting. It's a rule from which we don't deviate; but the conversation and invitation left women, marriages and heroes so mixed up in our mind, we could not untangle them, and therefore had to lay aside our quill. Well, well, Brown is actually going to marry! Poor fellow! he thinks the storms are over, and the matrimonial haven will be a bright, lovely, musical and eternal calm. The dream may be pleasant for a while, but oh! the waking, the waking, the waking! If he could just put it off and borrow our Linda a few months, we think it quite likely the marrying would not happen. Oh! wedded love, why

> "Art thou not, fatal vision, sensible
> To feeling as to sight?

A false creation
Proceeding from the heat-oppressed brain."

But may be *we* and Linda are exceptions to the general
rule, though *we* don't know why *we* should think so; for with
the exception of some "bilings" over on *our* part, we get along
as lovingly as other people—in fact, more so—a confounded
sight too much so. She is always running *to us*, with "what
a pretty this" and "what a comfortable that, Mr. So-and-so
has bought for his wife," and "doody, darling, don't you want
your old sweetness to go as well as the best?" Blast it, *we've*
a great mind to follow Brown and warn him not to marry.
And then our smoke house has got the chronic diarrhea; but
we dare not ask her to tote the keys or she'll kiss *us* to death—
no, she won't—confound your "us" and "wes"—I have to
bear it alone. It's *me* she'll kiss to death, and ask with a sickening whine, if I want my sugar-lumpshy-plumpshy-sweetness
to be taxed with such servile duties? Yes, I do. I want my
sugar-lumpshy-plumpshy-sweetness to—I want no sugar-lumpshy-plumpshy sweetness—pox take all finniken, sickening sugar-
lumpshy-plumpshy-sweetness. Women *may* do to marry, I
don't know about that; but let me warn mankind against
hitching in with any of this tribe of sugar-lumpshy-plumpshy
sweetness. I won't go a step to dinner—my stomach feels like
it is turned wrong side outwards. Oh, no, don't marry her—
she'd have Croesus himself hunting a poor house. If your
children (provided you have any, and ten chances to one she
wouldn't have any, just out of pure aggravation,) were crying
for bread, and your last half dollar but one was gone, she'd
propose to have them sent to bed—insist they'd rest better without eating any supper, and beg you to "please, my dear, sweet
sugar darling," (at the same time pressing your cheeks between
her hands and sucking your lips like a leech,) "run down to
the store and buy a bunch of artificials and four yards of
ribbon, to dress my bonnet,"—all to come out of one half
dollar. Now, maybe I'd marry again—yes, I would too; for I
verily believe some people have got good wives—plain, practical
wives—wives without kissing—without hootzy-tootzy talk—
wives who have some regard for their husband's purse. Oh,
yes, I'd marry again; but I'd have a marriage contract, ex-
pressly stipulating, that my wife was to be something else

besides a honey. Though I suspect I'm to blame. I informed
Linda before we married, that she was an angel, and the poor
simpleton has never quit believing I told the truth. I wish she'd
sail off to Heaven—I've a great mind to fly into a passion—
I'd swap wives with Socrates or any person else, and give boot.
I'll never marry another angel—not I—I'd rather be trans-
mogrified into a dose of ipecac. Angels do well enough in
their places; but they're not the proper kind of material to
make wives out of—at least they don't suit me—I want something a size coarser. P'shaw, why do I talk so? I'll never have a
chance to marry again. Linda won't die—she never catches
cold (and she can contract one as Mrs. Spriggins did by drinking water out of a damp tumbler,) or feels a pain in the side,
but a doctor must be called in, a bill run up against me and
"lubby"—that's what the foolish thing calls me—must hold her
head. But I bear it all. It keeps me poor in flesh, poor in spirit
and poor in purse; but I bear it all—bear all her fondling and
teasing and foolery—comply with the multitude of her childish
wishes and pass for a good husband. I'm a good hater—I almost
lose my temper sometimes, when I get to thinking on this
subject. Never mind; as soon as her father gives me my share
I'll change her tune. After that happy period—that glorious
beginning of a millennium, the store accounts, doctor's bills and
fondling, will grow "small by degrees and beautifully less."

But the hero—the hero! Where on earth have we left our
hero? We would as lief lose our baby, were we a woman, as
to lose our hero.

It will hardly be forgotten that at his last appearance his
feet were dangling in the stirrups—his body measuring its
length upon the ground and a weight, such as that which
haunts us when we have night-mare, pressing upon his lungs.
The dirk was moving towards his jugular with fearful impet-
uosity—the last hope of surviving the impending catastrophe
was gone, absolutely gone, and he had closed his eyes and
virtually consented for his life to go by default. But just as
the dirk was in the act of performing its bloody work, the
horse took a fright and started off, pulling him along. The
suddenness of this movement made the blade miss its aim,
and threw Squalls a somerset over the head of our hero.
But Fishback was out of one scrape into another—the horse

was getting faster, and Squalls pursuing and cursing him in a manner not calculated to retard his movements.

Fishback was now satisfied of the imminence of his danger in both directions, and acting under the influence of instinct he clutched a sappling with such force, that the girth broke, and the horse trotted away. At the moment he felt the girth break, he saw the unfeeling blade once more making its way towards his throat. This was unpleasant; in fact, it was quite annoying—to be fastened to the stirrups—the girth tangled, as it was, in brush—and then to be breathless and bruised from straining and jostling—and at such a time! it did look hard. And for Squalls to be whittling at our hero's neck vein, like it had been a piece of white pine, when he was surrounded by such embarrassments, really seemed unfriendly. But so it was, and so we are compelled to record it. As we stated a moment ago, Fishback again saw the dirk descending; he dodged the blow and grappled the hand of his antagonist with terrible energy. But he was much too weak for the ponderous and powerful Squalls. The hand was wrenched loose and again the gleaming blade descended, and once more our hero closed his eyes, as if resolved to be unable to testify if called upon about the manner of his own execution.

What a moment was this in the life of Fishback. There was no possibility that Squalls would relent and no chance for the blade to miss its aim.

But the combatants in their great excitement had failed to observe the arrival of a company of cavalry, several of whom having alighted pulled them apart, just in time to prevent a catastrophe, at the very moment when our hero's jugular was about to be ventilated.

Although scarcely conscious whether he was alive or not, Fishback by an instinctive principle in his nature, immediately resumed his wits—pulled his feet out of the stirrups, and asked for his horse. "Here he is," remarked a young cavalier; "I caught him for you." Our hero put on the saddle, fastened the girth, and mounted before the raving and infuriated Squalls had sufficiently recovered from the blindness of his rage to observe what was going on.

"Stop that infernal scoundrel; he's on my horse, and I'll swear I'll kill him this minute," thundered Squalls, as he tried to make his way to Fishback.

"Tie that man's arms behind him; I've borne with him as long as I intend to; tie him and lead him along," remarked the Lieutenant who commanded the company.

"Well but, Captain," said Squalls, "he's on my—"

"Shut your mouth—tie him—tie him. What command do you belong to, men?" addressing our hero.

"I'm discharged—jist a gwine to Winchester to see my brother—he was wounded at Sheppardstown. Don't know whar that fellar belongs; never seed him twe'll this mornin, when he kecht me and pulled me down, and tried to teck my hoss away. Here's my discharge."

After examining the paper the Lieutenant remarked, "you are a citizen, and of course can do as you like; but the army is retiring from the valley and it may not be safe to go there. You'll probably find your brother in Culpepper."

"Well, Lieutenant, I'll go back with you all—and as you're arter stragglers, I'll show you whar thar's one bout a mile from the road. He's a warin officer's uniform, and means to exert and go to the inimy." After this preliminary observation (delivered as they rode along, for by this time the company—with eight or ten stragglers they had picked up walking in front—had taken up their line of march,) our hero continued to paint and varnish the character of Slaughter, until he had decorated it with all the horrors of Pandemonium. A detail commanded by the second Sergeant and piloted by Fishback, was immediately sent forward to surprise and bring in the "so called" officer.

We will here state for the benefit of those who do not know how fashionable are *brutum fulmens* in the army, that when the order was repeated with emphasis and authority for Squalls' arms to be tied behind him, it had no other effect to cause the guard to hurry him forward to his place in the straggling procession, where strict silence and good behavior were enjoined on him in an impressive and somewhat threatening manner. In this way the company and its attaches wound slowly along, while Fishback and his companions loped forward to discharge their engaging and delightful duty.

Within half a mile of Stapleton's house they alighted, left a man to guard their horses, and moved around in such a manner as to flank the yard from every direction. Our hero told one of the men confidentially all about the bag of gold and instructed him to search for it in Stapleton's room who, he rightly conjectured, had furnished it as a bait, on the night of his steel-trap adventure. "Git it," said he, "and I'll slip it into my haversack twell night, and then we'll divide."

At length the little band grouped around the yard fence and Fishback coming to the gate spoke out, "Hello, Lieutenant Colonel Slaughter, I told you the Colonel can't do without you, and its jist so. He's on behind, and he sent me here with a squad of men to 'scorch you to the regiment." Slaughter had no time to reply, before the whole detail had surrounded, and were entering, the house.

"Come, lift your trotters outen this place, you dod-blasted-flop-eared-pole-cat," remarked our hero, while the rest of the squad by their looks were unmistakably seconding the proposition.

"Men," replied the captive, speaking sternly, "What right have you thus to approach a commissioned officer—I am here on leave of absence. Depart this instant. I will submit to no such diabolical indignities—depart—go—absent yourselves."

"Where's your commission," asked the Sergeant, somewhat intimidated by the position, tone and manner of the pretended officer.

"Don't let him show it," said Fishback, as he saw Slaughter pulling some papers from his pocket. "I know him—he rit it himself. Slaughter, stop pullin them papers and strike a trot, you cussed suck-egg puppy; you know you aint no officer."

"Here Sergeant," remarked the pretended Captain, "although you have no right, thus imperiously to interfere with my equanimity, or demand papers from an officer holding my rank, yet I submit them to your scrutiny with pleasure. As for this ruffian, Bill Fishback, as soon as you are satisfied with the examination of my commission, I shall avail myself of the authority my rank confers, to order him gagged."

"Very well, sir," replied the tender footed Sergeant, now satisfied of Slaughter's officership and uneasy about himself.

"He," continued the pseudo officer, "was caught in a steel-trap at this place night before last, while trying to steal a valuable horse from the proprietor, Mr. Stapleton. The agency

I exerted in his detection has made him resolve to wreak vengeance on me, and he has chosen this as a fit occasion, when he could get others to stand between him and the consequences. By unwrapping that rag from his left hand you will discover the print of the trap. Make three of your men gag him this moment."

Stapleton, who had been absent during the morning, now walked in and confirmed Slaughter's statements in the fullest manner. "Well, Captain, you must not think hard of us. Our Lieutenant sent us after you, with positive instructions, and *he* went by what this man told him," remarked the Sergeant.

"Yes, and I told him the truth; and I'll be blasted ef he shant go," observed Fishback.

"Sergeant, I've already ordered you to have him gagged. Don't let me have that order to repeat; otherwise your rashness in thus approaching an officer of my rank shall be productive of merited retribution."

"Very well, sir, very well," replied the pliable commander of the squad, "two or three of you take him and put a gag in his mouth." Our hero talked with urgency and rapidity, but the fiat had been uttered. The testimony had condemned him as a slanderer and a rogue. His power had departed and strong men grasped him, and were just going to follow instructions, when Charlie Webb, who had been examining the commission very closely, called to the Sergeant to suspend his order for one moment.

"This paper," said he, "is an arrant forgery. It makes this man Slaughter a Captain in the 4th Alabama. I know that's not so. I ought to know every officer in the regiment, as it hasn't been three weeks since I belonged to it. The commission is twelve months old and *I know* it's a forgery."

Slaughter's face grew pale, but he explained, "I am Captain of Company C, 44th Alabama. The mistake was made in granting the commission, and there has been no necessity for correcting it, for which reason I frequently report myself as Captain of Company C, 4th Alabama."

"You ought to have taken some other regiment," said Charlie; "the 4th and 44th are right alongside of each other. I know the officers of the 44th as well as of the 4th. You are not a Captain in either of those regiments. I know every officer in both of them."

"Yes, but I am."

"Yes, but you're a cussed, infernal liar," said our hero, who was now foot-loose. "I'me a gwine to tear them turkey tracks off of yore shoulders, you stinkin varmint." So saying he began to pull off the imposter's shoulder straps. This resulted in a struggle, during which several letters fell out of Slaughter's pocket, all addressed to "private John Slaughter, 9th Georgia regiment." The whole squad now joined Charlie in persuading the Sergeant, that he be made to take up his line of march, which was accordingly done. Slaughter again blended the sternness of official dignity with the majesty of pompous diction, but the Sergeant was no more to be overawed by these specious splendors.

"Men," said he, "if he don't start by then you can draw your swords, run them through him." Slaughter was subjugated, and having gathered up his blankets moved out of the gate.

Our hero's partner now privately placed in his haversack the bag of gold, and after they had made the distance of two hundred yards from the gate, publicly displayed a canteen of stolen whiskey and invited all hands to take a drink. Fishback proposed that every drink should be accompanied with a toast to Capt. Slaughter, which was accordingly done, with much merriment and many ridiculous cuts at him. After the last man of the crowd had drunk, he offered the canteen to Slaughter, who was reaching to get it, when our hero snatched it away, remarking, "Hit musn't larn no sich nasty, ugly tricks—they'l spile it." The cowed and conquered ex-Captain made no reply, but turned away.

Our hero had more than one reason for resolving to rid himself of his present companions. Something *might* grow out of the steel-trap story, and the future revelations of Slaughter and Squalls. Besides, if he remained with them until night, he would have to divide the money—a clear loss of three hundred and fifty dollars. True, it required great self-denial to surrender the privilege of seeing his two implacable enemies "grunt and sweat under a weary" load; but even that was fearful pleasure, since the sanguinary Squalls *might* do something rash at a time, when he was not closely watched.

He therefore—soon after they had reached the main road—

stopped as if to mend his girth again, and when the detail passed out of sight, took the opposite direction and traveled at a pace which soon put a quietus to all his apprehensions. Coming from the direction of Front Royal, he reached Culpepper in two days, after having been compelled to deliver his horse to the real owner at Gaines' Cross-roads, and foot it the rest of the way. To his infinite satisfaction, he learned at Culpepper that his command was camped about three miles off. He had really grown sick and weary of a rambling life. When not warmed by the immediate prospect of vengeance upon a powerless foe, his mind was tormented with such fears of meeting those he had offended, as made him pant for the protecting aegis of his company, as doth the jaded traveler for "the shadow of a great rock in a weary land." Feasting upon the prospect of meeting Captain Smith, repeating—that he might remember distinctly—the story cut and dried for the occasion, and chuckling at the innocence and guillibility of that officer, he hurried on through town. "None on 'em darsent to bother me, when he's about. He'll sarve 'em, like he sarved that feller as come atter his book-bag. I'de jist like to see Jack Graves or Squalls, or any on 'em. Slaughter, he's a coward. I'de like to see any on 'em drap in. I'de sic the Cap'n atter 'em. *He* wooddent growl round like Stapleton's dogs; he'd take hold. I'de ruther have him to purtect me as any yard dog in Amerikay. He *may* look a little cross when I git thar. Bound he tecks me to his bussum twixt this and night. I kin wind him right round my little finger."

"Hallo! Bill Fishback," spoke a voice from the shade of a tree near by.

"Why, Dick Ellis, howdy! monstrous glad to see you. Thought you'd retched the fur eend of kingdom come afore this. How on yeath come you didn't git whar you started?"

"Take a seat and rest yourself, and we'll talk these matters over more at leisure. Why haven't *you* joined the Federal forces, as you proposed to do?"

"I would take mor'n a hour to tell about it. Wait twell some other time. Seems like *you* ort to a got to em though."

"I couldn't. The Major's horse threw me and got away before I rode him a mile. I tried hard to catch him, but failed. I was just coming to my quarters when you and that fellow rode off—he has never come back since. The Major got *his* horse, but the Adjutant's has not been seen or heard from—that fellow and you are both considered, in the regiment, as thieves and deserters. You are charged with having taken off two soldiers, two horses and two valuable pistols. I expect they'll punish you severely."

"Not they, Cap'n Smith'll see em bout that."

"Capt. Smith has fallen out with you, himself. I'm the only friend you've got in the company."

"A trout cuddent pull a fishin line no strater'n I'll have him agin night."

"No, Bill, you'll never do that again, he's in the kinks too badly. The day you left he fell in with a fifty dollar bill, which he recognized as one of the bills he had missed out of his pocket-book when it was returned by Welch. The bearer, in stating from whom he got it, gave a very satisfactory description of you. This made him begin to think a little strange of your staying out so long, especially since the Major's horse had returned"—

"Shucks! I kin fix that smoother'n a smoothin iron."

"But wait, I am not through yet. The man who accused you of stealing his satchel and books came up afterward in company with an officer, and proved that he was not named Rufe Bates, and that he was a man of honesty, truthfulness and high respectability, after which he told a long story about your misconduct towards him. The Captain apologized, and promised that if he ever laid eyes on you, you should be severely punished."

"See ef I don't patch all that up fore I quit."

"Yes, but I have not finished. Rufe Bates is now on a visit to our Brigadier, who is his cousin. He comes over to see the Captain once in a while. I never heard what passed between them, though I don't suppose they've made any favorable remarks about you. They say Rufe's going to be our Adjutant-General."

"Dick, I'll give you ten dollars in gold ef you'll swear you wont never let nobody know you seed me here."

"What's the matter, Bill? Can't face the music?"

"No, don't mind that; but I'm not gwine about that infernal Rufe Bates. I'm afraid I'll kill him. Say, will you swear? It'll soon be train time, and I'm a gwine to Richmond."

"How're you going to git on?"

"Never mind, you swear; and then I'll tell you."

The swearing was duly gone through with, after which our hero informed Dick that he had obtained a discharge, and was actuated by no other motives than those of friendship in proposing to visit the Captain and his old companions.

"Let me see your discharge, Bill."

"Here, look at it, yore belly full! hit's ginnywine."

"Why Bill, you're forgetful—I was there, when this was granted, and took a match to it. You may pass guards with it, but don't show any such trash to Provost Marshals. They'll jug you sure as you do. Mine cost one of the regiment four weeks' imprisonment."

"May be this feller here won't look clost, least ways, I'll resk it." Then assuming a profound study for some minutes, he continued, "Dick, can't a feller git a passport to send his wife off on the cars, 'thout fetchin her up and showin her to the provo?"

"Yes, I reckon so."

"Will you come on and help me fix it, I'll give you another five."

A passport was soon obtained for "Mrs. William Fishback," the "s" ingeniously obliterated from "Mrs," and our hero armed with a proper passport launched out his V and got on the platform, just as the train was moving off.

The crowd on board was dense almost to suffocation. Fishback found himself compelled not only to stand, but that, under such a pressure from all sides as made it cramping and tiresome in the extreme. The restless spirit and versatile genius of our hero could not brook such restraints. Pushing and squeezing himself down the aisle, he looked anxiously to the right and left as if searching for either a vacant seat or an old acquaintance; until at length he came upon a young man leaning his head down in a manner significant of indisposition. "You're sick," remarked our hero.

"Ah, that I am, very."

"Lemme see your tongue," he continued, at the same time feeling his pulse. "Got the small-pox—got it bad—they put you in here to kill rebs. Yankee bullets can't kill em fast enough."

An uprising from all the contiguous seats, and a general

state of confusion began now to prevail. "What did you say, Doctor?" inquired every body.

"Oh, nuthin, nuthin, only jest a case of small-pox. Twon't hurt me. I've been nockalated; but I do despise to see people lettin soljers git killed up, jest by pure keerlessness." The platforms and the top of the cars were now crammed and crowded by a mass of men, hanging, swinging and piling together with an almost cotton-press compactness, while our hero deliberately seated himself near his patient in a comfortable, roomy and well ventilated position. The young man, tormented with a sense of his malady, "kept it before the people," that his was a case of small-pox, by the utterance of continued groans.

This happy state of affairs received no interruption. Fishback slept most of the way. Occasionally he would take a snack from the haversack of his patient, who was strictly forbidden to taste a morsel. The train had no sooner landed in Richmond, than the few who occupied the box in which our hero sat, were put under guard. A Doctor was sent for, the reported small-pox case turned out to be genuine, and the men thus put under guard were ordered into quarantine.

"Are they going to put *you* in quarantine, too, Doctor?" asked one of the passengers.

"Not atter I let em know about it," replied Fishback. "They mout though, I aint no army Surgint."

"Doctor, do you practice on the Mineral or Botanic system?"

"Some times one, and some times tother, and some times I jumble 'em up. Got any good chawin tubacker?"

"No, I don't chew. Have you any medicine with you?"

Our hero not precisely understanding the object of these questions, replied: "None ondly a little ligmy cognum, I carry along to cure the scours," after which he turned off.

At this time a number of soldiers marched around on either side of the car, vociferating the order to "move out men, move out."

"Yes, men," cried out hero, "git off, git off fast, or you'll spread it all over Richmond. I know how bad it is—had too many cases to nuss. Hit'll put you under the led of a coffin, ef you aint a leetle of the perticulerest. Why don't you hurry up there?" speaking to a slow motioned soldier. Then turning to the guard, he continued in a very commanding tone, "don't let none of em stop narry minit, for nuthin. I'm not a gwine to have no slow motions—a spreadin it." The men quickened their pace, the guard hurried them up, and Dr. Fishback walked leisurely to the American Hotel and engaged a room.

He now designed bidding Virginia a long adieu, for which purpose he went the next day and purchased a suit of fine clothes, and gave twenty five dollars for a bran new discharge. He also procured a passport for Mrs. William Fishback, to Albany, Ga., which underwent the same alteration as that obtained at Culpepper.

Two mornings afterwards Mr. William Fishback made his appearance at the Petersburg Depot, submitted his papers to the usual hasty examination, got a comfortable seat, congratulated himself on the turn events were taking, and looked out to enjoy a parting view of "the cloud-capped towers and solemn temples" of the Confederate Capital. It was not without regrets that he contemplated leaving the Old Dominion; but those regrets were largely overbalanced by the prospect of getting away from his unforgiving foes. There was nothing to bid him stay, excepting the recollection of joys too bright to last, of affections too earnest for endurance, and glories much too dazzling and meteoric to shine long. Like Wolsey, he had "ventured in a sea of glory" until "his high blown pride at length broke under him." The character he had established, the confidence he had enjoyed, the hopes he had cherished were all gone, and he felt it was time he too should go. Go to hunt other friends and profit by the experience of the past. The whistle blew, "all aboard" was sounded, and— Capt. Smith found himself accidentally ushered into the presence of his "Billy," just as the wheels rolled over and the train moved along. "Why, how de do, Cap'n," said Fishback, jumping at him, with fierce cordiality, when he saw there was no chance to elude his eye. "I'm so glad to see you, how de do," reaching out his hand.

"I want none of your howdies, you thieving scoundrel. What are you doing here?"

"Captain, you allers would bl'eve all manner o' things agin me. Taint no use o' my tellin you whar I been, and what

I been a doin since I left you. They offered me a discharge at Richmond, and I wouldn't have it, twell I got to Culpepper and heard how you was all abusin me, and then I come back—"

"You'r a liar! Nobody offered you a discharge."

"Well, but Captain, I done got it; here, see ef it aint all right."

"I shant look at any of your forgeries. It will be examined by the proper authorities in Richmond. What made anybody give *you* a discharge?"

"'Case, atter the Adjutant's hoss throwed me that night, I hain't had no use of my leg"—

"Shut your mouth! I wont hear another word from you. I know about your having any use of your leg. A man told me on the train yesterday of that steel-trap business, and there's the print of it on your hand. You had legs enough to prowl all over the Luray Valley, you rogueish, lying scoundrel. Hush! don't open your lips to me again. Conductor, send a guard here to take charge of this man. He's a deserter, trying to get home on a forged discharge."

Fishback and his guard were accordingly placed on the first returning train, and mailed to Richmond. Billy Weaver, the soldier whose especial duty it became to supervise the safety of our hero, was a kind-hearted, honest, mischievous looking fellow. Fishback read his character at a glance, but presuming upon the thickness of his wits, and impelled by the necessities of his own embarrassed situation, determined to try what virtue there might be in a golden bait. "Weaver," said he, "thar aint no use o' carryin me to Richmond; my papers is as good as Jeff. can make em."

"I don't deny that, but I must obey orders."

"No, you needn't, not when orders is wrong. Spoze they was to order you to shoot your own brains out, spoze you'd *obey orders*, would you?"

"That's a different thing."

"No it aint, no different thing nothing about it. What's wrong's wrong, and hit jest keeps a stayin wrong."

"Well, now, since I come to think about it, that's so; but how am I going to git out of guarding you?"

"I'll tell you 'bout that," remarked our hero, brightening up and speaking with earnestness and much unnecessary gesticulation—"you kin jest be a talkin to some other feller, and let me slip off, and ef you need a friend as kin help you along" (pulling out a handful of gold) "I'm hit."

"How much gold will you give me to turn you loose at Richmond?"

"Twenty-five dollars."

"That won't do, I'll ask a hundred."

"Well, ef you'l go with me clean off outen Richmond, whar thar aint nobody, and turn me loose, I'll give you a hundred."

"Can't do that, you'r a bigger man than I am, and you might tie me after you got me out there, and leave me without a cent."

"Yes, but I won't do it; I'll tote fair."

"Why not just turn you loose in Richmond? You'd as well trust me as me you."

"Well, ef you'll swear—"

"I won't swear a thing. I promised to carry you to town—and we are nearly there now—and you may git off the cars, I will not guard you any longer than till the train stops."

"But you'll put some other feller a foul of me."

"No I won't—"

"Pon your honor?"

"Yes, upon my honor, I won't interfere with you, or induce any one else to; but hand over the money quick, we're crossing the river." The gold changed hands, and soon the huge engine having crowded herself up among the numerous lesser ones surrounding the shed, and bellowed (as doth a cow at the sight of her calf,) came to a "full stop."

The cars were scarcely still before a Corporal came up the aisle, accompanied by a detail and several men under guard, and as he passed our hero, ordered him to "fall in behind." Fishback looked at Weaver. "It's all right. I've done as I told you. I won't interfere, nor induce any one else to. It aint my business. I belong on the cars. No doubt you can make the same sort of a trade with the Corporal, and for less money. He'll agree not to guard you further than the inside of Castle Thunder for fifty or maybe less—better hurry up, mister, there's a bayonet looking towards you."

The truth of this admonition becoming apparent, Fishback

hurried out, and after some delays, the whole group marched up and emptied into prison. Billy Weaver gave the gold to a comrade to be delivered to our hero before the key of Castle Thunder was turned upon him, but we have reasons for believing he never received it.

The confinement in prison and the breaking up of his calculations, were not near so terrible to Fishback as the prospect of having that lawless Squalls at any time turned in upon him—a fellow prisoner. From a dark corner, he watched eagerly every new comer, and felt greatly relieved as he observed each toting in of a strange face. His companions were by no means a desirable set, nor were the filth and stench of his quarters as well adapted to the style of his new harness as would have been the courtly chambers of the Graves Mansion; but, as the reader has had occasion already to learn, he was eminently a practical philosopher, and therefore, not less cheerful and composed in the one place than the other. He would play three handed seven up with Bob Dixon and Jack Stone—listen with seeming delight to the rickety verses of Joe Delton, or indulge in a game of stick-frog with the skillful John Carter. These were his chief associates, and he rendered himself the life of the circle—the happiest member of a "happy family." Bob and Jake were both confined for desertion. Joe, (who belonged to the City Guard) for—some offence, perhaps that of stealing another man's measure; and John Carter (a citizen) for the trivial mistake of penning and milking the wrong cow. Although these men were, like prison rats generally, without money—Fishback courted their friendship with no little assiduity, that he might secure aid in case the contingency before referred to, should happen. As we cannot linger long with these "boon companions," we insert, for the reader's accommodation, a specimen selected from numerous productions of the laborious Delton. One evening as they all lolled around, enjoying their respective amusements or idling away useless hours, he called for silence, and read as follows:

CONCERNING THE DESCENDANTS OF CAIN, RESIDENT IN THE SOUTHERN STATES OF NORTH AMERICA

"Once on one occasion really—Philips, Smith and Horace
    Greely,

With a "quaint and curious" hankering after sooty blackamoor,
Went to snorting and cavorting, and the glorious truth
    distorting;
Saying that the South was sporting,—sporting in their flesh and
    gore,
Echo sneaking, squeaking, speaking—spoke as she'd not spoke
    before,
        And she answered: "You lie, sure."

"They contended (so the term is) that beneath his epidermis
Cuffee was most white and pretty—full as pretty as a pink,
A most *lubly*, thick-lipped creature—fair and sweet in form and
    feature;
And in human scale, a bright link, only varnished as with ink,
Ink and charcoal ornamented, yielding a melodious stink
        Quoth the echo, "odious stink!"

"He's a mute, inglorious wonder—an illiterate son of Thunder,
And a scholar yet untutored, in the magic A. B. C.,
And we'll prove it in the sequel, that he is both free and equal—
Equal with us, as he should be, and—except his bonds—as free;
And although as yet, unheard of, still that he has great
    distinction,
        Quoth the echo, "dis stink shun."

"Esop in his nigger-fable, to convince us is not able,
That the Ethiopian cannot—cannot change his sable skin,
For it's plain to naked eyes, he's a white man in disguise;
Yes, our own beloved, worshipped, cherished dark complected
    kin,
He's our almost more than brother—ah! in good sooth, he's our
    twin,
        Quoth the echo "Sour twin."

"While they thus were cogitating, and their thoughts and
    feelings stating
On the nigger's wrongs so shocking—suddenly there came a
    knocking,
Knocked he like his fist was leaden; ope'd the door and thrust
    his head in,
'Twas a nigger—northern nigger—the Manhatten island, bred in,
Raised to eat 'thout any victuals, and to sleep 'thout bed or
    beddin,
        Only this and nothing more.

"He essayed then to address them, in a manner 'twould distress
  them,
Stating, proving how he's suffered by an unforeseen event,
Suffered, though he'd done his duty—honest if his skin *was*
  sooty,
Acting faithful, fair and generous whereso'er in life he went,
Now left by capricious Fortune sans a solitary cent,
   Quoth the trio, "let him went."

"He possesses vast presumption, to think we, for home
  consumption,
Keep a love that can be lavished where the distance aids the
  sight,
Where the nation and creation may behold our situation,
And up-lift us to a station, proudly, luminously bright;
Avaunt, ye home-made nigger—quick, avaunt, and quit our
  sight."
   Quoth the echo, "quit our sight."

  "That's a regular ripsnortin good hyme," observed Fishback. "Hit's what you mout call a real buster. You got it outen
sumthin else besides that lousy lookin head of yourn."
  "He got it outen a dicshunery, I seed him," remarked the
witty Dixon, "and I'll lay, ef he had a dost uv ipecac, he'd puke
up a whole raft of books—book-shelf and all."
  "I wonder," said a dirty-faced fellow, (whose name has
escaped us) "how long that thing stayed in him. It's curious
he didn't git salivated."
  "Delton," resumed Fishback, "You've give out the hyme,
now whar's the sarment? Come, blow yore nose, and pitch
out—tex, sax of the 'postules—six verse. Come, blaze away."
The poet, abashed by these unappreciative demonstrations, returned to his quill, and the rest to their previous employments.
  Fishback had now made his last public appearance at Castle
Thunder. The next morning he was sick, and on the day
appointed for his trial, an ambulance conveyed him to the
pest-house, a wretched victim of small-pox. He was borne
thither after dark. In one corner of the room assigned to
him and his co-sufferers burned a dim light and near the bunk
on which he was stretched, sat two of the nurses, engaged
in low conversation, which seemed to have been interrupted
by his arrival. "As I was saying," continued one of them,

"when I went for the gun to shoot Mrs. Lane's beef he leaped out of the door and ran with all his might, leaving a horse, bridle and saddle, and a knapsack full of very decent clothing. This was the strangest freak I had ever witnessed. From Mrs. Lane's he went on to my father's, where he was taken sick. Having proven by a system of bogus testimony, that he was a wealthy and highly respectable Georgian, just elected to a seat in the Legislature, he induced my father, by the basest misrepresentations, to sell his whole possessions, except the negroes, for a mere song. He was promised a settlement on the unoccupied lands of this arch-deceiver, and informed that he could purchase rich cotton-growing lands in the wire-grass sections of Georgia for greatly less than the price his own had sold for. After he thus sacrificed his property, my father gave a farewell party to his neighbors on the eve of going South under the guidance of his villainous pilot. The news of these rich Georgia lands had reached me, and I attended the party, determined if Fishback, (for such was the name he bore) would promise me the prospect of a good investment, I would sell out also and go with the family. But I didn't get a chance to confer with him on the subject. He no sooner saw me approaching the house than, driven by the same strange infatuation, he jumped bare-headed from the window and ran off, leaving several hundred dollars and one or two other articles of value. I was prepared to form a most favorable opinion of him, and, even after recognizing him as the same man who had behaved so remarkably at Mrs. Lane's, his forged recommendations read so flatteringly, but little explanation would have been necessary to have rendered me the dupe of his unprincipled machinations. Twice he fled from me without a cause, but now that he has brought my father's family to poverty, when next we meet I shall feast my knife with savage pleasure upon the hot blood of his heart." Clenching his teeth, he continued. "I hardly feel like I could spare the corpse of a wretch so impious."

Our hero, though racked with pain, heard every word of this conversation, which continued beyond what we here report. The torments of his mind greatly aggravated the virulence of his fever. All night long the sympathetic Jack Graves sat by his bunk, nursing him with a woman's gentleness and anxious solicitude. About sunrise he brought him some medicine. Our hero had fallen into a light slumber. "Wake up," said Jack, "I have got you a dose of physic; its not hard to take, it will improve you." His eyes at this moment met those of poor Fishback, who looked imploringly submissive. "Humph!" grunted Jack, as he drew back the cup and turned away. Other nurses ministered to the wants of Fishback from that time on.

The warfare between a vigorous constitution and an obstinate disease, continued day after day, until at length consciousness faded into dim twilight, and disappeared in the night of irrationality.

The last words that fell upon his ears before a knowledge of passing events forsook him, possessed a strange and dreamy familiarity. They came from a newly arrived victim of the prevailing contagion: "Doctor," spoke the voice, "without a successful administration of discutents, this malady will inevitably result in mortuary consequences."

"Mortuary consequences, mortuary consequences, mortuary consequences," were the receding thoughts of our hero as his mind clung to the objects of sense, and yet fluttered to be loose. These words were the straws at which drowning consciousness caught in her struggle to rise.

THE END.